CAT
TALES

Endorsements for *Cat Tales*

Cat Tales *will not only give a fun fresh look at God's nine spiritual fruits through the eyes of these nine cats, it will give you a chance to know Teresa's heart for bearing fruit by living out the gospel of Christ.*

I've known the Herbic family for years, and they all have a huge heart for the rescue and adoption of God's living creatures, both feline and human.

Enjoy the fruitful journey that Teresa is going to take you on!
~ Jim Landers, Family Pastor,
Pleasant Valley Baptist Church, Liberty, Missouri

🐾 🐾 🐾

Cat Tales *is a beautiful story that relays the fruits of the spirit in a new way though the lives of nine unique cats. More importantly, it is a glimpse into the very special heart of the Herbic family that deeply honors God's call to care for orphans.*

I pray that this book will challenge you to live your life for Christ and to look for ways each day to learn more about God's lessons in the fruits of the spirit.

~ Kimberly A Wilson, Awana Children's Ministry
Commander, Pleasant Valley Baptist Church,
Liberty, Missouri

CAT TALES

Nine Cats, Nine Lives, Nine Loyal Spirits

by Teresa J. Herbic

Ambassador International
GREENVILLE, SOUTH CAROLINA & BELFAST, NORTHERN IRELAND

www.ambassador-international.com

Cat Tales

This is a fictional work, however, all stories are based on actual cats that were adopted by the author's family over a 45-year period of her lifetime. Names, characters, places and incidents either are the product of the author's imagination or are used fictitiously. Any resemblance to actual persons, living or dead, events or locations is entirely coincidental.

© 2013 by Teresa J. Herbic

ISBN: 978-1-62020-215-9
eISBN: 978-1-62020-314-9

Cover art and illustrations: Kaysha Siemens
Cover design and typesetting: Matthew Mulder
E-book conversion: Anna Riebe

AMBASSADOR INTERNATIONAL
Emerald House
427 Wade Hampton Blvd.
Greenville, SC 29609, USA
www.ambassador-international.com

AMBASSADOR BOOKS
The Mount
2 Woodstock Link
Belfast, BT6 8DD, Northern Ireland, UK
www.ambassador-international.com

The colophon is a trademark of Ambassador

Dedication

Thank You first to Our Lord and Savior Jesus Christ
Who died on the cross for our sins,
Who loves us and His precious creatures, too!

Cat Tales is also dedicated to my family which
includes faithful prayer warriors and friends.
A special thank you to the nine cats featured throughout
this book that my family adopted over the past 45 years.
They remind us about God's love and patience
through simple warmth and kindness.

God bless precious orphan children and
animals still needing homes.
May they find forever families!

*For Jesus says, "I will not leave you as orphans;
I will come to you." (John 14:18, NIV)*

Table of Contents

Chapter 1
The Spirit of Love: Meet Prince   9

Chapter 2
Joy: Introducing Dakota   17

Chapter 3
Peace: Sharing Lolli's Story   25

Chapter 4
Patience: Here's Precious Puff Ball   33

Chapter 5
Kindness: Serving up News about Sampson   41

Chapter 6
Goodness: Meet Cutie   47

Chapter 7
Faithfulness: Here's Sister Tootie   55

Chapter 8
  Gentleness: Now, Roxy   63

Chapter 9
  Self-Control: Finally, Brother Rootie   71

  Conclusion   79

Chapter 1

The Spirit of Love: Meet Prince

MY NAME IS PRINCE. I'M a heavy-weight Bombay tomcat with dense, black fur all over me, and I sport a bit of gray hair next to my whiskers. Don't we all grow gray at a certain age?

I once was a wandering city boy. Then, my owners decided to move, so they took me to the country. They insisted they couldn't keep me; therefore, I found myself dumped in an unknown land.

I was tearfully discouraged, but had to keep a positive mindset about the situation. So, I picked my large, able body up from the ground and moved toward a brighter day.

Some intriguing humans caught my eye. They sat together on a wide-open lawn. I spotted an adult slick-haired mutt nearby who was napping. I noticed from the corner of my eye another cat covered in colorful, thick, extensive fur. She looked friendly. Three squirrelly gray kittens sat at her side.

I also noticed a small, spirited red dog chomping its jaws coming toward me. Believe me, her bark sounded bigger than her bite. I disregarded her bravely.

I pressed on to meet what I had decided was my new family. I walked respectfully, yet assuredly, up to them. I trudged past an impressive white porch swing and a couple glasses of iced tea awaiting thirsty lips.

I put my best paws forward, and then moseyed as they did in Wild West, except I poured on the charm without saying the customary, "Howdy partners!" The family warmly smiled as I passed through.

So, I waltzed over again. I thought I'd rub next to them if I got the nerve. I stepped firmly across the yard. Then, I strolled between the people. They all looked at me and laughed because I avoided the barking dog like the plague.

The third time I passed, I had the courage to swipe one of the kids on the back. It was a little boy. I think they called him Raymond. He turned his head in a twitch and grinned from ear to ear.

I stood there for a moment in the middle of the group observing everyone. I made a few more passes, and then plopped down for a while to relax.

Next thing I knew, a little boy and girl were petting me like I was the coolest cat ever. I rubbed and caressed against them.

The pretty lady of the house stroked my hair—it felt incredible. They soon named me: Prince. I reveled in sharing affection with others in this animal and people kingdom.

I attempted to warm up against one guy, the dad of the house. He didn't appear interested in cats.

I thought: *I'll love him more, later.* Regardless, I felt assured this was where I belonged.

That night I cautiously investigated my surroundings. I found a patio underneath a deck to rest, so the rain wouldn't soak me. I tried lying next to Rusty, but he seemed annoyed and distracted. So, I sought a soft, red rug for coziness. It goes nicely against my black, Italian fur.

I felt relaxed and glad Rusty let me lounge on his patio. We had a festive dinner out there. He ate from an old skillet; I ate politely from one of the cat bowls.

The other cats congregated with their mother in the big cat house. The yapping little dog, named Dusty, had her own area to eat and sleep.

The two kids in the family returned curiously to check on me—I really liked that. They even pet Rusty and Dusty's heads a little.

I felt good about the home. So, I planned to stay a very long time.

The next day, I woke up to a lethargic rooster crowing awkwardly at the crack of noon, precisely.

That's ridiculous! I thought.

There were also a few chickens in a pen area. All they did was to eat and sleep. What a life on three-acres of extraordinary land!

I engaged blissfully with Puff Ball's three gray kittens— they were comical, chipper cats. They liked to run and catch bugs. I playfully trained them about new hunting tactics.

On a track through the back woods, we stumbled upon a creek. Rootie didn't seem aware of the water; he kept his eyes fixated on a sparrow instead. As he gleefully ran ahead, he tripped tragically. When he plunged deep into the frigid water, he gasped for air frantically.

We all panicked. I quietly said a quick prayer because I couldn't let him drown. I instinctively dove into the icy cold waters and swam rapidly to Rootie. I grabbed the fur on the back of his neck with my timid mouth.

I swam briskly back to shore against the rapid currents. I thought we were goners for a moment. Then, I voluntarily—with God's help—swam again. With all my might, I moved toward shore with the kitty; both of us panted for air.

Rootie spit out a large amount of water. Thankfully, he seemed alright, yet terrified. We all thanked God and rallied home.

Dad came out to do some yard work. I rubbed against his leg a few times. Next thing I knew, he stroked my head—I could tell he loved me. He really felt concerned for our well-being.

I'd made a breakthrough with this otherwise dog man. Now, he called me prince of the kingdom, too.

I felt tired after everything that had happened, so I sought a silent resting place. I considered the fact I might discover more inside the house. As I moved into unchartered territory, I found a comfortable green chair.

I hopped on it while Dad sat in another recliner. The kids and Mom relaxed on the couches. It was a perfect, peaceful nap. I relished in the love and togetherness.

As days and months went on, we lit the fireplace in the chilly temperatures and gathered in the living room. We loved each other's company, cuddling and caring for one another and delivering occasional kisses.

During the daytime, I appreciated my animal family hopping throughout the yard. Rusty didn't move much, but Dusty energetically roamed. She was a spunky little dog with an earsplitting bark. I loved jogging next to her. Sometimes, we even raced across the yard to see who ran the fastest.

Puff Ball, was a sweet lady with a patient, calm kitty personality. As a calico cat, she had yellow, gray, and white fur. She liked to hang out with me when I took it easy in the yard.

Otherwise, I was always moving about with her kittens, showing them the ropes. I felt like an uncle to them. I just wanted them happy, safe, and to experience love and adoration.

The girl of the family liked sitting and petting me. She called me a handsome prince, and made me feel exceptionally important. She talked to me like I was a person. I felt I could run and be anything I wanted to be with the love I had found.

I could rub this family's legs and hang out with them forever. I learned in hard moments as long as your heart is full of love, one must courageously love with all he or she is. This way, you always discover true purpose. This time, in my efforts, I found love to last forever.

Memory Scripture

You must love the Lord your God with all your heart, all your soul, and all your mind. (Matthew 22:37, NLT)

Chapter 2

Joy: Introducing Dakota

MY NAME IS DAKOTA. I'M a broad-shouldered, short-haired tiger kitty. My story begins in the arms of a toothless woman outside a department store.

I was in need of a home. This lady kept asking everyone

to take my brothers, sisters and me with them. I felt miserable as I watched my siblings go. Yet, I felt happy for them to have a home.

As the only kitten left of the bunch, I also wanted a family. Finally, a lady and her cute Asian daughter saw me and couldn't stop googgling over me. I could tell they really liked me. So, I lifted my soft white paws out of the lady's arms, preparing to lunge into their arms.

The Asian princess smiled at me. I felt hopeful my tiger face, baby white paws, and tiny raccoon tail would steal their hearts.

Who knew I would be adopted that day? I hadn't planned on it, but it was love at first sight for me, the lady, and her petite toddler princess. As they agreed to adopt me, my heart filled with joy and excitement. I sensed a genuine adventure ahead.

We proceeded inside the store. The nice lady held me tenderly in her arms as if she already loved me. While purchasing kitten food and necessary items, I snuggled next to her like a newborn cub, purring and basking in her essence.

We drove home to share the news with other family members. We hoped they would embrace me, too.

On the ride home I tip-toed all over the back seat. I

kept rubbing back and forth against my new sister as she sat in a funny-looking car seat. I loved her already and felt joy just being around her. I kept purring while my new sister giggled at my kitty moves.

When we arrived at home, and they took me inside the two-story modest home. I hit the carpet running to check out my new pad. I met my new daddy for the first time. He looked tall and handsome.

I thought Daddy's office seemed like a playground. I wove in and out of the legs of the desk and chair. I slid on the floor mat and repeatedly stroked against every family member; I could hardly contain myself!

🐾 🐾 🐾

Have you ever felt this type of closeness? There's nothing better!

🐾 🐾 🐾

With energies running high, I played all night until rest time. Then, I curled into a fresh pet bed with my new puppy sister, Mitzi. We looked like a couple of fur balls all fluffed up. Mitzi's really old and appeared almost like a mother to me. We felt comfortable as a family snoozing together.

The next day, I awakened to a velvety hand petting

me. I jetted off on the carpet for another fun-filled day. I discovered jingle bell balls my family provided for me to bat around. Mitzi rolled around with me. I even toppled over her. Not sure she agreed with that!

That day, my family officially named me Dakota. It's an American Indian name which means: friend. I am a friend indeed. My middle name became William for the mascot Willie the Wildcat because he is a feisty little comrade like me.

As years went on—my adopted sister, and Dad kept supplementing my name. They did so because they saw the relevance in my interests. You know those hyphenated names these days? They are nothing compared to my name which grew increasingly more extensive.

Dakota William Hunter. Hunter was added because hunting in is my DNA. I have mastered running, jumping, and hunting for fun, little treasures.

Dakota William Hunter Hachi. Hachi became part of my name because of my loyalty to family. Hachi means loyal and faithful friend.

I cherish my family. I'm most pleased being in the middle of the family circle. I like to look around and see my mother, father, and sister. Sometimes, I lay on my Daddy's newspaper or my mother's writings. It's my way of blessing them.

I'm so glad my family cares for me. They feed and pet me. They hold me in their arms like a buttercup. Most of all, they love and help me discover new things.

During the years, I've learned tricks you don't often see cats perform. I can say, "Out," when I want to go outside and roam. I have my own cat door to exit whenever I'm ready. Then, I go to a window and meow when I'm prepared to come back indoors. My cat door gives me a stellar headache sometimes coming inside it, but it's a convenient option.

I say "Ham," when my tummy craves a tasty treat. Ham is what they give me when I'm an especially good boy. The taste is smoky, juicy and remarkable.

I play peek-a-boo out of my red pet tent. My family views my green emerald eyes peering in and out of the tent. I even close my eyes when my family prays. That brings me joy and peace. It comforts and encourages others.

At the start of the day, I like to join family for breakfast and prayer time. I usually plop down right next to my dad. He even lets me climb his chest. He scratches my chin and rubs my fur. I can't get enough!

Sometimes I get a little stir crazy indoors, so at night I go outside for long walks around the neighborhood. I've had a few scary times, but most of all it's just plain fun.

My regular route is fulfilling every evening. I hunt for insects and other animals. I've made friends with most cats, like Whitey, Clyde and some beautiful girl kitties who are just enjoying life.

I got attacked by a raccoon one time. That felt unpleasant. Other than that, my journeys are always joy-packed. I'm pretty much a social butterfly as some say. I'm not a big people cat, but I delight in meeting other animal friends and being with my family.

One day, I dashed onward to a wild excursion. I mistakenly took a wrong turn and saw a drain ditch. I felt tempted to enter. So, I skirted inside, while testing the normal boundaries. The darkness and mystery terrified me. I became very anxious.

Then, all of the sudden, I plummeted into a ghastly mud hole. I jolted up and ran straight home covered in filth. My daddy saw me and lifted me into his brawny arms.

He gave me a soapy bath and I felt brand new. This reminded me life can be messy, but it's what we make of it that matters. Being joyous is a state-of-mind, an element of maintaining a good attitude in Christ. My family realized joy in Jesus.

It seems God often answers our prayers when we really trust and believe. He has satisfied me with the right people to adopt me. I will always be taken care of and loved. There's regularly a surprise around the corner.

Recently, I welcomed a new brother home. My mother and father adopted a little boy named Braxten. He has big cheeks, a cute face, and a hilarious laugh.

God gives us all we need. Having Him in our lives is the greatest joy of all.

Memory Scripture

Shout with joy to the Lord, all the earth! Worship the Lord with gladness. (Psalm 100:1–2, NLT)

Chapter 3

Peace: Sharing Lolli's Story

MY NAME IS LOLLIPOP, BUT people call me Lolli. I'm a black and brown Toyger cat, wearing a leopard body.

Life for me began in a midwestern town. I lived my first years there in a no-kill animal shelter. I'm glad the shelter cared about me and other animals, keeping me alive, well-fed, and loved. Constant hope flowed inside me. I knew someday something great would happen!

One day, the shelter manager placed me into a pet travel carrier. A few other furry friends came along, too. I couldn't tell where we headed, but I felt peaceful—everything would turn out remarkably.

Along the way, I heard someone say, "We're moving to a pet store in the city."

I thought, *that sounded terrific!*

Some of the scaredy cats scratched and clawed at the doors of their cages. A few hissed and meowed in loud commotion. I didn't want to cause any grief, so I kept quiet, trusting in my Heavenly Father.

We arrived shortly thereafter. The shelter manager conveyed her love for us, and a desire for all of us to be adopted. Next, they put us in a storefront together; however, in separate cages.

My dwelling included a bright green rug, a generous food dish, and a water bowl. Two pleasant ladies and a gentle guy took care of me. They retrieved us at night to play with, and pet, us. I seemed to get extra attention because I kept things uncomplicated and peaceful.

Days went by, even weeks. I couldn't tell how long I had been there. Although countless people viewed me and tapped on the front glass, no one adopted me. I still had this confident belief inside me God would find a way.

One day around Christmas time, a family arrived that had two adopted children. I immediately felt drawn to the daughter. They kept calling her Mei Mei. She stood at my area for an extensive period. She looked at me constantly: talking, reassuring, and providing smiles. I wanted so badly to leave with her right then. Yet, I knew I must keep calm.

Finally, Mei Mei resolved to ask her parents about adoption. I heard her tell them, "Lolli is all I ever want for Christmas!"

The lady at the pet store added I had been there for many months.

"As an older cat, Lolli might not get adopted," she stated.

I saw love in Mei Mei's eyes. Soon, the rest of the family stood gazing lovingly through the window.

Before I knew it, they freed me from the cage. Then, Mei Mei and her dad came in to visit with me. I appreciated every moment with a gentle hug here, a pat there, and a swipe of my body against their legs with each turnaround.

Then, the parents assembled for a talk. Next thing I knew, they completed some paperwork.

A good indication, I thought.

Mei Mei remained optimistic the whole time.

Next, they rescued me from the enclosure and carried me to be held by Mei Mei's precious arms. I felt so pleasant and comfortable inside. Mei Mei's father and mother paid for my adoption. They shopped for some extra cat food and materials. Then, we travelled home in five quick minutes away.

My first look of the home proved delightful. I had never seen a habitation as significant and bright.

There must be hidden treasures and pockets everywhere.

They settled me inside Mei Mei's room along with cat food, litter, and water. It appeared a superior apartment; it felt spacious and comfortable. I had two cat beds in there. I slept in one at first. Then, after a few trips under the bed and dressers, I hopped to the bottom of Mei Mei's bed and rested there for a while. She didn't seem to mind.

I woke up refreshed and alert. Mei Mei opened her door, and we set out to explore. I weaved in and out of furniture, checking all rooms and closets. Mei Mei and her brother, Braxten, created amusing playtime toys with feathers.

We travelled for an unbelievable car and truck ride over the next few days. We drove on the major highways and streets. I maneuvered all over the vehicle.

I saw flashes of people and buildings going by. I felt an indescribable serenity and adventure in my spirit.

When arriving home, the urge came over me to explore the big house all night. However, Mei Mei's dad—my grandpa—told me to return to Mei Mei's room.

Not without a challenge first, I thought.

I felt like a real risk-taker. I flew out of the room and under the couch. As Grandpa's big hands reached after me, I scurried down the stairs to the basement. I felt concerned about what was in the dungeon, so I flew back up the upstairs.

I ran a few more laps out of bounds. Then, I eventually gave in and went to bed. I decided I'd rather sleep with Mei Mei, anyway. I needed to resist the temptation inside and resolve to better behavior. Making my family unhappy didn't feel good inside. On occasion, however, I still jet down the hallway in my quickest gallop simply for the exercise factor.

On the weekends, Mei Mei's parents—my grandparents—set up walkie-talkies to communicate. The kids had some late night fun time in their rooms while their parents watched a movie.

Mei Mei and I lounged in our room watching television cuddling, reading, assembling puzzles, and listening to the radio. I loved watching the television flicker back and forth. I also liked the quiet tunes on the radio.

When we needed something, we buzzed the walkie-talkie to talk with Grandma Teresa and Grandpa Galen. That seemed cool! I could hear their voices coming across vividly. They assured me I belonged. My mother and I—and her pint-sized stuffed puppy, Lilly—settled in nicely.

I gained an easy-going manner. I didn't desire any trouble. I felt the heart to be with my family and enjoy every waking moment. I am a happy, wise, and calm cat. There existed a real peace inside me, especially when we pray.

Each night we gathered in the living room I sat on Grandpa's chest delighting in a head rub and meaningful attention. He read the Bible and Grandma recited the fruit of the Spirit passage in the book of Galatians.

Then, we went around in a circle to pray over people listed in our family prayer jar. I like when prayers are answered because everyone rejoices!

I am thankful to share my peace with each member of my home. I am often reminded of my humble beginnings; no matter what, I always believed God had a plan for me. This is His plan I am living and adoring each day!

🐾 🐾 🐾

When we trust in the Lord, our peace should indeed surpass all understanding in our minds and beings. I pray we will always have this peace in our home.

I pray for you, too, as my story is read. I pray God will bless you with His transforming peace! As the following scripture is read, remember God has all of the answers if only we focus on Him.

Memory Scripture

Then you will experience God's peace, which exceeds anything we can understand. His peace will guard your hearts and minds as you live in Christ Jesus. (Philippians 4:7, NLT)

Chapter 4

Patience: Here's Precious Puff Ball

HI, MY NAME IS PUFF Ball! What a great name for a cat, huh? I'm a classic Calico gal.

As a baby, I stood out from my siblings with all my fancy colors. Unlike other kittens, I am a designer cat. I cherish my spots as I consider them God's gifts.

Yellow, gray, and white,

You see me day or night.

That's my special rhyme!

My family chose me distinctively from a large litter. They had never seen a Calico cat before. I felt honored.

I rode home with them in a two-door, classic Monte Carlo. I had never seen a car like it before. What a sweet ride!

The kids held me in the backseat and chatted the entire ride. They looked at me, talking to me like a human being. They pet me all over and scratched my neck just *pu-r-rfectly*. They even told me I was beautiful, I felt like their one and only.

Arriving at the homestead, I studied the layout. The kitchen connected to the living room which came in handy. The living room featured a television and a small pool table.

Now, that's entertainment! I thought as I knew [the pool table] would add amusement for years to come.

There was a sliding-glass door in the room leading to the great outdoors. There was a patio immediately by the door—convenient for quiet relaxation. I spent most of my time there or in the yard. I loved the open air.

A well-mannered dog named Rusty dwells here, too. He's a stocky guy who sometimes looks a little disparaging. He's no threat to cats. He's just a mellow fellow.

My first years had a steady routine until one day I decided to race inside to be with family. I noticed the sliding door shutting ahead of me. I wanted so desperately to be in from the cold, so I made a mad dash for the living room. In the midst of my run, I found myself slammed painfully into the sliding door.

I'm trapped and ruined forever, I thought.

My brother and sister immediately felt frightened for my life. They laid me on a soft blanket and tenderly stroked my head.

They transported me right away to the local veterinarian who mended some of my wounds. I hurt all over, inside and out. I felt an anxiety as if life would soon end.

As I laid there limp and lifeless, the vet seriously explained to my family I might not make it. I felt destroyed in many ways. Still, my spirit prompted me to live.

To share my mild encouragement, I lifted my head ever so slightly. I couldn't bear death. I wanted to show my keen desire to heal. My brother, Ray, and sister, Teresa, begged and pleaded to care for me. Each day they visited me in the building out back where I stayed while recovering. They prayed for God to heal me. I felt their love like never before.

Often, I vomited every bite of food. I could hardly keep anything down. This immensely concerned Ray and Teresa, and, frightened me, too. Then, I remembered a scripture the family once taught me which states: "Be anxious for nothing, but in everything by prayer and supplication, with thanksgiving, let your requests be made known to God" (Philippians 4:6, NKJV). So, I remained calm and patient while attempting to regain life.

Patience became a constant requirement as my healing didn't come quickly. I was sick and disabled for about a year. My family continued to care for me with extra petting, love, and grace. Not once did they give up on me even in the extended mending period.

Then, finally one day I began to feel like my former self again. I felt invigorated and inspired to rise up. Then, Ray and Teresa came in to check on me, to demonstrate my new strength.

I lifted one paw after another until I stood on all fours. They shouted with glee and leaped with joy! They couldn't believe it . . . I couldn't either. We all celebrated with sheer bliss believing my livelihood would soon be restored.

"Praise the Lord!" They said. "We have a living breathing

Calico cat again!"

Each day, I gained more energy. I began to feel fully rehabilitated. I cherished every moment, knowing I was now a miracle cat. My family told everyone about God healing me.

I felt inspired to achieve many great things! I share a passion and zest for life, reminding everyone to appreciate our blessings.

I even spent extra time with our dog, Rusty. I rested next to him on the patio. I communicated with gentle meows and encouragement. I prayed for him to be happy and fulfilled. I could tell he enjoyed my company. He even smiled slightly to show he felt better.

Then, not long after my transformation, I met a handsome stunning neighbor cat with long gray fur and loving, intentional eyes. We fell in love at first sight. After a few months of courting, we married and gave promises to be together forever.

Before long, I became pregnant with kittens. I discovered pregnancy isn't easy. I started feeling nauseous again and feverish. Sam, my husband cat, felt concerned for me, and so did my human family.

They wondered if I could really carry kittens to term after my accident and lengthy illness. The extensive pregnancy wore on me, yet I remained patient until the birth of my babies.

The time came when I began to have labor pains.

Pain, again, I thought. *Not good!*

Then, I felt they were coming. One-by-one, despite the agonizing suffering, I endured for my babies. They looked beautiful—all three of them. They became my pride and joy!

They're every bit worth the wait!, I thought.

Ray and Teresa named them Cutie, Tootie, and Rootie! Rhyming names seemed appropriate for a rhyming cat. I felt so grateful God pulled me through the earlier tragedy.

Through time and sustaining patience, I was healed by the hand of God. I've lived a happy, long life giving birth to kittens of my own. What a blessing!

Rusty adopted them as special kitty nephews. He looked after them, sleeping next to them as their protector.

As years have flown by, I've had fun times as a mother. Sam and I watched the kittens grow. They each had their own unique personality. They had to individually learn about patience and long suffering in their own ways. Thanks be to God for helping them!

Now, I hope important meaning is found in my story. Whenever we feel like giving up, we must hang in there. For God is always working. He has the power to do anything if we praise, thank, and pray to Him consistently while waiting patiently for His answer!

Memory Scripture

Be anxious for nothing, but in everything by prayer and supplication, with thanksgiving, let your requests be made known to God. (Philippians 4:6, NKJV)

Chapter 5

Kindness: Serving up News about Sampson

I'M A TUXEDO BILLICAT NAMED Sampson. A Billicat is a black and white breed of cat with thick shimmering fur. Some people say my patterns resemble a cow's. Obviously, I'm not a cow, I'm really a cat!

Recently, I joined housemates Puff Ball and Rusty in a friendly Missouri homestead. My parents, brothers, and sisters recovered me as a stray. They generously took me into their home. They loved me instantly and gave me all I needed. I'm quite thankful.

I spent my days playing gleefully with the kids, Ray and Teresa. They designed homemade outfits for me. They dressed me ridiculously funny— I never knew what I'd appear as from one day to the next.

I imagined me on the catwalk displaying their awkward creations. Not sure they would go over too well. Between you and me, I don't want to hurt their feelings.

Ray and Teresa lugged me all over the place in their tiny arms. They regularly let my body hang in the balance. It wasn't always comfortable, but I liked it because I knew how they felt about me. They really loved me, and I couldn't picture being anywhere else.

When inside: I sprawled out on their children's books and papers, taking an occasional glance at the ads and photos. When outdoors: on sunlit afternoons I napped idly on the porch with my furry friends. It was a massive porch with enough room for a table, chairs, and an outdoor grill.

There was freedom to roam. Ray and Teresa rode their tricycles around the porch in circles while I pursued them, meowing at their every move. I tried to hop on the back of their bikes; however, I never seemed to hit the mark. They thought it was hysterical.

Some weekends, they put on their Native American headbands, banged on their drums, and rode around like Indians. I pretended we are the three little Indians. I envisioned us living on a Native American Cherokee reservation. By night fall, we had a powwow; a *paw*wow as I like to say. There, we formed a circle, chanted, and gazed at the stars.

I visualized it as Indians danced years ago. I tried to meow like they sang in tribal regiments, but I couldn't quite grasp the language. Dynamic energy and excitement filled my head. I had quite the colorful imagination!

I read once some famous people in history owned tuxedo Billicats. People like William Shakespeare and Beethoven. Imagine being the cat of a famous author and poet like Shakespeare. I'm not sure I could have kept up with his writings. Maybe I could have contributed some-how to his plays.

Imagine traipsing around Beethoven's place listening to symphonies in the making, or high stepping across his grand piano. It might have really hurt my ears with the amplified sound. Who knows? I might have composed the greatest symphony of all: "Cat Concerto Number 9."

Also, I heard Beethoven's first name is Ludwig. Imagine calling your owner Ludwig? That's extreme and a little out there! Besides, I heard Ludwig didn't get along so well with his family. That doesn't sound appealing! Ever hear the grass is greener . . . ? Doubtful!

Regardless of all feline opportunities, I would rather have lived right here with my chosen family. I stumbled upon them by God's grace, of this I am sure!

My family was great! We liked our solid spiritual foundation. We often prayed to God, not for rain like the Indians, but for other things like health, peace, kindness, and love.

This one period of time, though, wasn't so peaceful for me. My typical rowdy human brother experimented with me as the guinea pig. I felt uneasy as he latched me to a rope and lowered me like a pulley into a large black waste can.

I squirmed and shrieked until our sister came to release me. I couldn't believe the tension it caused. I prayed the situation never occurred again. I knew my brother was playing, so I forgave him. I demonstrated only the purest kindness in return. It felt best.

I learned more about kind manners. Like how a male cat, like me, should always let ladies go first. Sometimes I feel like speeding out in front of them, but this behavior isn't respectable. I've also realized the courtesy of cleaning up one's own area. When I spilled milk or food on the porch, I always tried to clean it up.

I felt most successful when I'm being a good friend. When I saw someone happy or sad, I tried to relate with them. Whatever the situation was, I was always at my family's side. I've learned if you don't expect anything in return, many times one gets so much more in life.

One time I shared affection with a stray cat passing through. She came along on Christmas Eve to visit our home. We fell in love with her as a remarkable long-haired white Ragdoll cat. She truly looked beautiful.

Ray and Teresa pointed her out right away and brought her in for milk. I offered her some of my food on the porch when she came out. She tilted her head ever so gently against mine to let me know her appreciation.

My family called her Snow Ball, and we all accepted her as if she might stay. The next day it was Christmas. We enjoyed amazing company. We snuggled up to her and made her feel welcome. We desired to get to know her, so we offered her a special warm, pink blanket. I shared one of my mouse catnip toys which are my favorites.

We gave her treats which we all shared graciously. They seemed like the appetizers for our pre-dinner. We had a gourmet meal together complete with chicken pate and vegetables. My brothers and sisters gave her many pets and back rubs.

By evening, she had disappeared. Our family thought she must be some sort of angel cat because of the way she came and went so quickly and touched our lives.

I hope I touch people's lives, too. As a gentleman cat, I always strive to do what's right. When God tells us to share and be kind, it's our duty to follow. I hope you will be kind and follow, too.

Memory Scripture

In his kindness God called you to share in his eternal glory by means of Christ Jesus. (1 Peter 5:10, NLT)

Chapter 6

Goodness: Meet Cutie

HELLO, FRIENDS! MY NAME IS Cutie! I am one of three solid gray, American-shorthair kittens. I look like a Russian Blue cat with a silver tone, only I'm not from Russia.

My mother is a Calico with all sorts of colors. Somehow, my brother, sister, and I turned out totally gray. We are the three baby kittens our mother delivered. You may have heard about us!

When other kitties are naughty in my sight, I do all I can to refrain from such activity. Although it's challenging sometimes, I strive to do what's right even in the prospect of temptation.

Do you ever experience temptation?

My brother, Rootie, regularly faces some sort of dilemma. He's an unruly youngster who climbs into mud pools and splashes when it rains. He smiles mischievously because he likes to drench us. We feel miserable, wet, and dirty.

He also enjoys the dirt, collecting it bountifully on his fur. Maybe that's a boy's way, rambling in the muck?

I'm not into appalling behavior. I'd rather exist in quiet accord. My sister is harmless. Tootie is a good friend and a faithful sister. She often helps my mother, and she prays for us when the going gets tough.

I like hanging out with her each day and exploring the countryside. I love the beautiful flowers on the lawn and the trees we're learning to climb. I benefit from just being together.

It seems if I don't have the answer about something, I can ask my sister, brother, mother, uncle or any of the other animals. Then, I learn the how tos of surviving in the wild kingdom.

Some think survival is all about being savage and tough. A cat's basic instinct is to hide or be outright gallant and defensive. I believe survival stems from the goodness in ones heart. When we are good to others over time, they will naturally accept us and care for us in return. I delight in the goodness that comes from loving, caring relationships.

I adopted a dog to become part of our family. He was a senior citizen named Rusty; he was a fifteen year old mixed yellow Labrador Retriever who really needed a friend. Often, he would lie on the patio for hours, even days at a time without moving.

I felt sad for him and resolved one day to designate time to be with him. We just laid there. He knew I was harmless. As we hung out together, I moved increasingly closer to this big fellow. He never barked or growled at me.

I felt encouraged to lounge with him. My human family often petted him and tried to encourage him, too. I could tell they loved him, and they loved me. They just wanted what's best for us. I felt optimistic about drawing our family nearer to God.

With every move, I got closer. Then, on one occasion, I landed right next to Rusty's tummy. I felt the urge to plop my head right on top of his soft gentle tummy, so I did. He felt comforted with me being there. I could tell because he didn't moan like he had in instances before. Instead, he slept peacefully. When he woke up, he gazed affectionately at me with his big brown eyes as if to say thank you.

The nature of cats and dogs is to generally not get along. Often cats scratch dogs, or slap their paws at them in fear. Dogs bark and bite cats if they feel threatened in any way. That's where the expression "fight like cats and dogs" came from.

Maybe cats don't like it when dogs are referred to as man's best friend, or the fact they are sometimes chased by dogs for entertainment. Chasing can lead to a predatory outcome not pretty for a kitty! The obnoxious behavior gets a dog nowhere.

Cats don't like the harassment. Some cats fear dogs and simply won't approach a dog for anything in the world. They feel it's better to be safe than sorry. Cats can also be solitary and non-social. They tend to reign in dominance.

Although dogs are often the aggressor in these relationships, on some occurrences, the cat is the bold defender. Cats crave attention, and there can be occasions when a cat will simply not tolerate the dog embarking on their territory. Cats are territorial, marking their scent to show whose boss. They often go to the extremes defending their territory.

It all comes down to obedience and functioning like a healthy family. The best thing to do in any situation is to get along with one another. It's better to make friends than enemies. It's better to be non-threatening and social. It's all about slow, cautious introductions and becoming familiar with one another.

In my experiences with dogs, Rusty was simply a good ole' boy—he was even-tempered and somewhat lackadaisical. I felt free to wander and explore all around him. I would have been a fool not to warm up to him. Our visits were peaceful, our intentions were good. That's what I call companionship!

There were moments, however, when I needed some play time. When I got my energy up, I would rise to do a little kitty dance for Rusty. It was as if to say, "This one's for you, champ!"

Rusty sat up all perky and grinned. That reassured me I was making progress. I knew he didn't quite understand me completely. He looked at me funny when I raised my ears and tail. That was my way of telling him, I was trying to be friendly. When he wagged his tail, he was happy. When I wagged my tail, I was not so happy.

As Sir Walter Scott once said, "Cats are a mysterious kind of folk. There is more passing in their minds than we are aware of."

So true, Sir Scott, so true! I was always thinking of and considering those around me.

When I was restless, I usually went on escapades with my brother. He was the busy bee in our family.

He, my sister, Uncle Prince, and I went to the clearing at the bottom of the hill near the well. We liked to watch the four wheelers pass by on the trail. Usually, we saw our neighbor, Rodney, and my brother, Ray, on a Suzuki blazing.

When we returned, Mom fed us. Our human parents fed us, too. I knew it helped Mom. I tried to give her a break more often because I sensed she really needed one.

My mother always cleaned my siblings and me after dinner. We didn't like water baths, so we relied on our mother for grooming us. I was sure her tongue got worn out from the abundance of work. Some day we need to do this cleaning on our own.

Did you know cats spend approximately one-third of their time awake cleaning themselves?[1] That's some serious personal hygiene, folks!

As we all know, however, life isn't always spotless and sparkling. It gets messy sometimes. There were days when I felt frisky and liked causing some ruckus. I have had to call on God for answers and direction in those situations.

Nevertheless, I tried and do my best to persevere myself as a good little cat, sharing the lesson of goodness with my kitty and human friends. Are you seeking and searching, too?

Memory Scripture

Call to me and I will answer you and tell you great and unsearchable things you do not know. (Jeremiah 33:3, NIV)

---

1   Random History.com, "99 Interesting Facts about Cats," http://facts.randomhistory.com/interesting-facts-about-cats.html.

Chapter 7
Faithfulness: Here's Sister Tootie

I AM TOOTIE, CUTIE'S YOUNGER sister. I came into this world just a few minutes after Cutie.

I love my family and pray for them every day. It may seem silly, but it helps us in moments when we need it most. My family often calls me Sister Tootie like a nun, except

I'm just a kitty.

If I was a nun, I would pray each day at the chapel. I would rise up early and pray on my knees for good things to happen. I would share joy with everyone and show them love. If I were a nun, I would bow down late at night and pray with my sisters for the world to see God's faithfulness and understand the depths of His love.

Even though I'm not a nun, I figure I can still share God's love day and night. I can show people I care. I can tell people about how much God cares. I can pray in full trust because I believe God can do anything! Nothing is impossible for God!

One day my kitty sister, brother, and I found ourselves in a strange area of the country. We felt timid and couldn't find our way home. It was spine-chilling in the woods, and we had been out there for hours.

The day became night. The light soon extinguished into darkness. Our eyes become watery. Our bodies became weary. Even so, I kept faith God would pave the direction for us to make it home.

In the wooded tree line, we could hear what sounded like a pack of wolves howling. The sound grew increasingly louder. It echoed deeply as if the pack was moving in more closely. Looming in the darkness, gray wolves lived and fed in groups. It seemed as if there could be hundreds of them.

The thought of a gray wolf sinking its sharp, pointy teeth deliberately into me didn't resonate as a pleasant engagement. So, we crept quickly, yet cautiously away from the dreadful noise.

We thought we saw a black shadow in front of us. It looked as if there were three animals before us. We guardedly tiptoed through the limbs and dirt. Then, we realized how foolish we were as it proved to be our own silhouettes.

We imagined what must be rushing through our tender mother's thoughts. How frantic she must be. How worried and terrified she was to lose her precious kittens.

Then, we thought of our human family—our brother, sister, adoptive mother and father. They loved us very much, too. I know they must be praying right now for our safe return.

When I thought of all of the happy times we had already shared, I realized how much God has really blessed us. I remember Ray petting me constantly and just hanging out with us animals. It was almost as if he was one of us. He was somewhat rowdy like my kitty brother.

I recall Teresa was talking to us as if we could speak English. We began meowing back and attempting to repeat the language of humans. It was as if we could fluently relate to one another.

Our understanding of love initiated from being open and caring for one another. Our relationship was not simply a surface one. We truly sought one another's thoughts and opinions. We didn't hide what was on our minds. We didn't pretend to be anything we were not. That means a lot to me.

When a family can pour out its heart in full faith—without fear of expectations, games, or manipulations—this is what family is intended to be. We were always there for one another; trusting God to keep us pure in His love. We didn't make trouble for each other or cause family grief or drama. It was the kind of devotion God is all about. Thank You, Jesus!

As these loving thoughts remained in my mind; still, the darkness revealed lurking concerns. Repeatedly, the eerie sounds of the night daunted. In the neck of the woods, we heard footsteps. Second-by-second, the thud of an animal's hooves pursued us.

In every instant, our hearts raced with fright. As the noise continued, we hid behind a large oak tree, eager for protection. I said an immediate prayer in my head, and a white-tailed deer darted right pass us. It was a large buck with massive antlers and a heavyweight body. I don't think he noticed us.

The echo of nocturnal insects twittered in the night. A barred hoot owl screeched exceedingly as if to pierce our ears. Its distant calls were familiar. Yet, we heard great horned owls hunt domestic cats. They stalk late at night, perch high in a tree, and watch attentively with their huge, determined eyes.

Owls have powerful binocular vision. Their sensitive, sharp, and feathered ears transmit a neurological signal. This indicates there's a snack below. They, then swoop down suddenly upon their prey. They can carry animals equal to their body weight.

They might envision hunting some unguarded kittens like us, I thought.

Since our mother wasn't around, I knew we could be in serious danger. The notion of it gave me the heebie-jeebies! Then, my brother's faint whisper into my ear scared me tremendously; I jumped back. My sister screamed, my brother grabbed my paw in desperation, and I asked the Holy Spirit to be with me. Then, peace returned.

My sister cried out, "What should we do?"

My brother sobbed.

I responded in the only way I knew, "We must pray!"

As we knelt together on our tiny kitten paws, we felt a

rush of hope within us. We heard a faint meowing call in the wind.

"Who could that be?" we questioned.

Then, we realized it sounded like mother.

"Meow, meow!"

A cat call recognized. It indeed sounded like our mother. We started trotting along cautiously, so we did not trip over the woods before us, but quickly enough to reach our destiny.

We looked left and right to avoid missing her. Then, straight ahead of us, there stood our gorgeous Calico mother.

Although it stayed dark, we could see her feline figure faintly in the night. The reassurance had arrived and our prayers had been answered.

In kitty unison, we exclaimed, "Praise, God!"

God had brought us home after we prayed together. There, waiting for us, our family: Kitty Mom, Prince, Rusty, Ray, Teresa, Mom, and Dad. So, we celebrated God's gift, declaring His Glory and answer. Thank You, Jesus!

As the morning came, we realized the purpose of our being: to proclaim God's unfailing love and faithfulness in everything. Even in the times we are lost, God finds and brings us home into His care. We are thankful and blessed!

We give God the honor . . . our Holy God!

Memory Scripture

It is good to proclaim your unfailing love in the morning, your faithfulness in the evening. (Psalm 92:2, NLT)

Chapter 8

Gentleness: Now, Roxy

I am Roxy. I'm an American Curl kitty. Have you heard of American Girl dolls? Well, I am an American Curl doll! My hair is long and gray with a fancy feline appeal. My ears curl ever so slightly. That's why they call me an American Curl.

Adopted from a local pet rescue, I am thankful to have a home. I started out with some major medical troubles. In my pain, I try to display gentle, loving behavior even when I'm suffering.

My first health scare initiated from ear mites. Do you know about ear mites? I didn't realize anything about them until my ears started hurting and itching rashly.

Ear mites are tiny white insects living inside of the ear canal. They stay there until they are removed. They are very contagious.

Since I came from the local animal shelter, there was a chance another animal had them. They examined me pretty good; at times it was hard to see them.

I wanted to cry loud meows, but did my best to refrain from doing so. Instead, I gave warmth to my new parents, praying to distract myself.

My family came to see me at the shelter and fell in love with me instantly, as I did with them. Thankfully, they adopted me. Then, the veterinarian told them he wanted to check me thoroughly for the adoption paperwork.

He took one glance inside my ears and felt dismay. He reported not only about the ear mites, but also about an ear infection originated from them. He found some white pus and inflammation in my ear canals. He prescribed some effective medicine drops to rid my ear of those creepy, crawly creatures, so I could feel better.

Then, I travelled home. I respect my adoptive parents and family; we were each other's true best friends and companions. I liked sitting on the arm of their lounge chairs, my favorite spot. I also sat on my mother's shoulder, rubbing her neck serenely.

She adored me although she had allergy issues, causing her to sneeze. She didn't complain at all. She simply sanitized and, without hesitation, held me.

My parents potty trained me with newspapers in a box. That was where they set me to go poo poo pee do when it was time. They also bought me a big litter box which is cooler than the newspapers. That was for my use when I finished potty training.

I got a little unruly whenever they pulled out my cat fishing pole with the pink feather attached. I'd never really been fishing. So, I pretended the feather was a small fish with pink scales.

I imagined it swimming rapidly through the sea, and me going after it like a deep sea diver. I might have even swam like an Olympic swimmer to snag it. The thought gave me a belly-rolling laugh; I toppled right over. I batted at it with my paw. Regardless, it was good clean fun!

When I finished batting practice, I perch on the window sill where the sun would shine bright and warmly upon my fur. I leaped up in a giant bounce, finding it fairly easy to make the jump.

Did you know cats are able to jump five times their height in one leap?[2] It's true!

Once I made it up there, I gazed out to see what activity is going on. Some days, I saw squirrels climbing trees and gnawing on acorns. Other days, I saw red and blue birds nesting.

There was often a mother bird swarming in to feed her babies a worm or two. My parents even placed a yellow birdhouse just outside the window. It had a small ledge where the birds came to feed.

What a glorious sight! The birds and other animals didn't seem to mind me staring out the window. As I wondrously gazed I found myself beginning to doze off into a southern siesta.

---

2   About.com, "Cat History and Domestication," _http://archaeology.about.com/od/domestications/qt/cat.htm_

Ever play hide and seek?

As my nap was ending, I headed to my hiding spot in the bedroom closet. There, I found all sorts of ridiculous toys such as tunnels, mazes, strings and balls of yarn, and a great feline lounger. I love to explore.

To remain stimulated, I did my exercises in the closet. Did you know a cat's back is incredibly flexible with up to fifty-three loosely-fitting vertebrae?[3]

I did some paw stretches, lifts, and back bends. Then, I raced through the upper hallway to share my feline athletic skills. My mother once read cats can travel speeds up to thirty-one miles per hour, so I have a mere record to beat![4] Wouldn't that be something!

I wore myself down some days, especially during the winter. Not long after my first birthday, I developed another infection; a feline upper respiratory infection (URI).

I was sneezy and had watery eyes. I also had some gunky

---

3   Random History.com, "99 Interesting Facts about Cats," http://facts.randomhistory.com/interesting-facts-about-cats.html.

4   Ibid.

stuff in my nose that made me feel miserable. My parents transported me to the vet for treatment; I was placed on some tetracycline medicines for about ten days. Within this time frame, I started feeling better.

I felt joyous to return home to heal completely. My mother held me, devotedly comforting my soul. I felt blessed and truly loved. I rubbed against my parents' legs to mark my territory.

I thrived being inside with my family. I never really desired to go out like other cats I knew. I never pictured me hunting or rambling in the yard. Even so, I looked forward to my daily gawking out the window. I guess I was becoming far too civilized in my indoor society.

🐈 🐈 🐈

Speaking of domestication: did you know cats first became domesticated in Egypt? About ten thousand years ago, the Egyptians initially thought of us as effective exterminators, but then they realized their personal need for our friendship.[5] People from Egypt loved their cats so much, if anyone took the cat and attempted to smuggle it out of the country, the act was punishable by death.[6] Basically, cats

---

5   Ibid.
6   Ibid.

found themselves protected and cherished by their owners.

Known for its ancient civilization and pyramids, Egypt is the largest Arab country. Imagine being there and the song "Walk like an Egyptian" playing in the background.

From Egypt, cats spread to countries all over the world. My parents are not Egyptian, but I'm sure they would like to know this information.

How about you? Do you have an Egyptian cat? Have you ever adopted a cat? Can you walk like an Egyptian? Why don't you give it a try . . . have fun!

I'd love to hear all about what God has done in your lives. Write me sometime; I'd enjoy reading about your journeys. It's fascinating to hear stories of love and tenderness.

I especially treasured being with my adoring family. I shared my affectionate, calm behavior with them. It encouraged others to be gentle, too.

God always has a plan for us. Although, I went through some tough illnesses, I persevered in Christ. Now, I'm thankful God had given me a magnificent home—a place to share gentleness.

Memory Scripture

Since God chose you to be the holy people he loves, you must clothe yourselves with tenderhearted mercy, kindness, humility, gentleness, and patience. (Colossians 3:12, NLT)

Chapter 9

Self-Control: Finally, Brother Rootie

Hi everyone! My name is Rootie. I'm Cutie and Tootie's younger brother. I'm known as the rowdy one. I sometimes lack control—a real wildcat. I desire to run and play all day. That's my primary mission in life: to play as my human nephew, Braxten, would say.

Behind our two-story home, lies three acres of a mystical jungle. There are hundreds of shrubs, trees, plants, animals, insects, and a long winding creek. I imagine it an oasis, also prime hunting land.

My Uncle Prince taught me to hunt.

Did you know cats are native hunters? It's part of our innate instinct and behavior. I sense it in my being.

🐾 🐾 🐾

I loved when Uncle Prince said, "Let's go hunting!"

Some of the things we hunt for are: mice, rats, birds, rabbits, roaches, scorpions, and grasshoppers. During our runs, I learned all about small animals to chase after—apparently, it's okay as long as they're not poisonous.

One day, we discovered a tiny gray mouse. Here's what happened:

Uncle Prince spotted the mouse by a large maple tree ahead of us. We halted in our tracks. After all, it wasn't hunting if we didn't sneak up.

Prince told me to stand quietly behind a wild, shrubbery bush. The plant looked small, but it was extremely dense—I easily hid behind it.

When Prince meowed the word, I crept up slowly and

quietly on the mouse. Then, I had a knee-jerk reaction to fly forward. I scared it off in a panic. Prince told me I should have remained patient and not been so abrupt in my chase. If I waited a little longer I could have caught him; maybe next time.

I rested that evening and dreamed kitty thoughts. Hunting birds and animals filled my mind. The next day, I sprang up like an unruly jackrabbit and ate a mild breakfast. Then, I flew over to Prince's palace.

I asked him, "Prince, how about another shot at hunting?"

He thought about it a few moments, and then told me to ask my mother first. I ran back home like white lightening to ask her. She said it would be all right as long as I remained careful. So, I galloped like a brave lion back to Prince's palace.

He asked, "Well?"

I said, "Let's go!"

We set out for another wild animal kingdom adventure. I felt determined to find the mouse I saw yesterday to show him who was the boss.

I sought him by a tree, under bushes, in the meadow for what felt like forever. I never saw a trace of him. Then, out of the corner of my sage green eye, I thought I spotted a black rat snake near a brush pile. It had a slimy dark body with a white neck and a fine-pointed yellow tail.

Ew, a black snake! I thought.

Then, excitement filled me intensely. I could hunt the snake like a lion stalking his prey.

Here's the vision:

> I belly up to the back of the brush pile near the snake. I daringly leap ahead and successfully take the snake into my possession. It's like starring in an action movie as the stunt cat.

I couldn't believe the spectacular feat I was about to pull off:

> I sprint home anxiously with the slithering snake in my mouth thinking all the time, *what a tree-topping trophy!*
>
> "Okay, then. I'm about to show this baby off," I said to myself.

Prince didn't seem to pay full attention. He thought I had my eye on a mouse instead, so he kept his distance. So, I put my plan into action. I quietly and patiently snuck up behind the snake. I maintained my self-control even though the anticipation encapsulated my brain.

I was positioned right next to him. Then, I launched my paws on top of him like a lion snagging his prey.

Self-Control: Finally, Brother Rootie

I pinned him down like a wrestler. I took his neck firmly into my mouth like a saber-toothed tiger. Then, I sprinted rapidly up to Prince.

I about knocked his Bombay socks off. He literally fell over right there.

I laughed inwardly and shook my head as if to say, *"Come on! Let's go show everyone our distinctive catch!"*

I ran like the whistling wind toward home. I didn't see my family at first, so I figured they were napping in the dog house. I rushed over to it and dashed inside.

"Meow . . . Wahoo!"

My mother and sisters exclaimed in fright. They looked in shock with the funniest expression I ever saw in my life. It all felt worth the fiasco, although I know it wasn't the nicest thing I placed in our home.

Soon after, I dropped the snake ruthlessly to the ground. My family leaped back to avoid the slimy reptile. Prince tried to apologize to my mother.

After her shock alarm deactivated, she calmed down and understood. She never forgot my prize snake trophy, that's for sure. No one would.

Next, I flew to my sisters asking what was on the agenda for the day. They told me it was time to see what the twisting creek was all about. We met Prince and

asked him to take us.

Gymboree! I love this country life! I thought. I couldn't be-lieve all of the astonishing adventures to do each day.

I flew ahead of everyone, so I could be first to the creek. When we got there, I couldn't believe the shiny, glistening water. I noticed my reflection in the water.

While my sisters and Prince bumbled about, I couldn't resist climbing on the rocks by the creek bank. *What fun!* Then, the amusement ended. I abruptly slipped into the creek waters. I couldn't catch my paws, so I went straight into the water, head first. It felt icy and extremely cold against my fur. I couldn't stand it.

I screeched, "Help . . . help!"

I thought I would surely drown. Then, all of the sudden, Prince jumped in after me. As I gasped anxiously for air, and continually plunged under the water, Prince grabbed my neck in his able-forced mouth and swam me to shore. I praised God in my soul while unloading many slurps of water from my throat.

Thank You, Jesus, I thought!

"Thank you, Prince," I said in my softest, most humbly defeated meow.

I learned that day I needed to be much more cautious and careful in all situations or I could die. Even if I survived,

like I had, I could be terribly hurt. Thankfully, however, God protected me and returned me home to safety.

Subsequent to my constant rowdiness, I uncovered the fruit of the spirit referred to as self-control. It is what I needed all along.

This spirit allows me to be secure and happy. I have to maintain control of my body and be a more patient cat. I can still run and have fun, but there are certain boundaries and rules I need to abide by accordingly. I'm glad I know this now.

Memory Scripture

Better to be patient than powerful; better to have self-control than to conquer a city. (Proverbs 16:32, NLT)

Conclusion

GOD's WORD READS IN GALATIANS 5:22–23: But the Holy Spirit produces this kind of fruit in our lives: love, joy, peace, patience, kindness, goodness, faithfulness, gentleness, and self-control. There is no law against these things! (NLT)

This scripture in the book of Galatians reminds us God has specific characteristics He is always working to instill in our beings. As the sheep and kitties of His pasture, we are obliged to follow His teaching.

I pray, as an adoptive mother of many spirit-filled cats over the years for you to consider adopting a kitten or cat as well. Maybe you have already? If so, good for you!

May God bless you in all you do as you seek His good will and the fruit of the spirit in your life! May you experience many more cat tales and inspirational adventures.

Good night and happy adopting!

For more information about

Teresa J. Herbic
&
Cat Tales

please visit:

Email: familiesforadoption@kc.rr.com
LinkedIn: www.linkedin.com/pub/teresa-herbic/12/8aa/b07
Blog: http://cattalesfruitofthespirit.blogspot.com/

....

For more information about

AMBASSADOR INTERNATIONAL

please visit:

www.ambassador-international.com
@AmbassadorIntl
www.facebook.com/AmbassadorIntl

Best Easy Day Hikes
Orange County

Help Us Keep This Guide Up to Date

Every effort has been made by the author and editors to make this guide as accurate and useful as possible. However, many things can change after a guide is published—trails are rerouted, regulations change, facilities come under new management, etc.

We would love to hear from you concerning your experiences with this guide and how you feel it could be improved and kept up to date. While we may not be able to respond to all comments and suggestions, we'll take them to heart and we'll also make certain to share them with the author. Please send your comments and suggestions to the following address:

> The Globe Pequot Press
> Reader Response/Editorial Department
> P.O. Box 480
> Guilford, CT 06437

Or you may e-mail us at:

> editorial@GlobePequot.com

Thanks for your input, and happy trails!

Best Easy Day Hikes Series

Best Easy Day Hikes
Orange County

Second Edition

Randy Vogel

FALCONGUIDES ®

GUILFORD, CONNECTICUT
HELENA, MONTANA
AN IMPRINT OF THE GLOBE PEQUOT PRESS

FALCONGUIDES®

Maps by Daniel Lloyd © Morris Book Publishing, LLC

Library of Congress Cataloging-in-Publication Data.
Vogel, Randy.
  Best easy day hikes, Orange County / Randy Vogel.—2nd ed.
      p. cm.—(Falconguides)
  ISBN 978-0-7627-5107-5
  1. Hiking—California—Orange County—Guidebooks. 2. Orange County (Calif.)—Guidebooks. I. Title.
  GV199.42.C220738 2009
  917.94'960454–dc22

                                          2009002492

Printed in the United States of America
10 9 8 7 6 5 4 3 2

Contents

Map Legend.. ix

Acknowledgments.. x

Introduction... 1

How to Use This Guide... 7

Ranking the Hikes.. 8

The Hikes

The Coast... 10

1. Bolsa Chica Slough Trail.............................. 11
2. East Cut-Across to Moro Ridge Loop 15
3. Laurel Canyon–Bommer Ridge Loop..................... 19
4. Dilley Preserve Canyon–Mariposa Loop 23
5. Little Sycamore Canyon Trail 27
6. West Ridge, Lynx, and Cholla Trails....................... 31
7. Valido Trail 35

The Foothills 38

8. Telegraph Canyon Trail via Rimcrest Entrance 39
9. Weir Canyon Trail Loop 43
10. Santiago Creek Trail Loop 46
11. Peters Canyon Lake Loop 50
12. Borrego Canyon to Red Rock Canyon................... 53
13. Live Oak Trail.. 57
14. Riley Wilderness Park Loop....................... 60
15. West Ridge and Oak Trail Loop 64

The Mountains 68

16. Silverado Canyon–Silverado Motorway 69
17. Santiago Trail 73

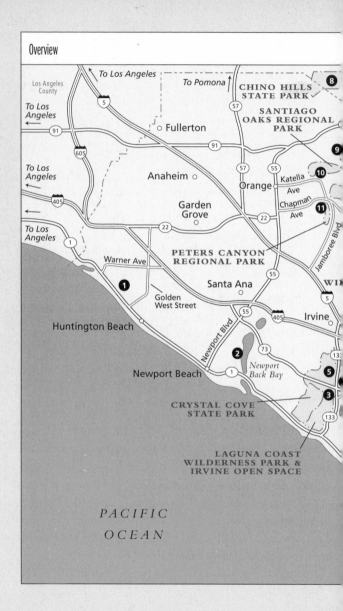

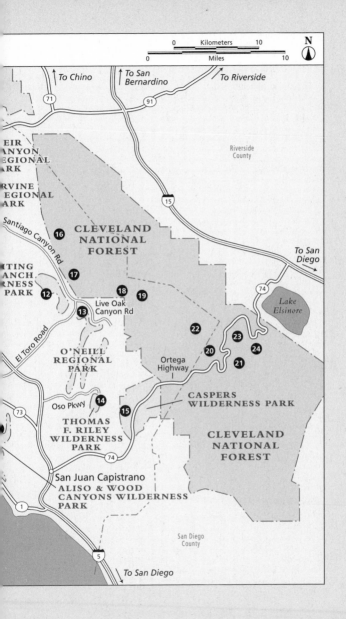

0   Kilometers   10

0   Miles   10

To Chino

To San Bernardino

To Riverside

71

91

Riverside County

15

EIR ANYON EGIONAL ARK

RVINE EGIONAL ARK

Santiago Canyon Rd

16

CLEVELAND NATIONAL FOREST

To San Diego

17

TING ANCH RNESS PARK

12

74

Lake Elsinore

18   19

Live Oak Canyon Rd

13

22

23

24

El Toro Road

O'NEILL REGIONAL PARK

20

21

Ortega Highway

73

Oso Pkwy   14

15

CASPERS WILDERNESS PARK

THOMAS F. RILEY WILDERNESS PARK

74

CLEVELAND NATIONAL FOREST

San Juan Capistrano

ALISO & WOOD CANYONS WILDERNESS PARK

1

San Diego County

5

To San Diego

18. Holy Jim Trail 77
19. Trabuco Trail 81
20. San Juan Loop Trail 85
21. Bear Canyon Trail 88
22. Los Pinos Peak 91
23. El Cariso Nature Trail 95
24. Morgan Trail 98

About the Author 101

Map Legend

═(90)═	Interstate Highway
═(30)═	U.S. Highway
═(20)═	State Highway
═[41]═	Local/Forest Roads
= = = =	Unimproved Road
- - - - - - -	Trail
▬▬▬▬▬	Featured Route
—··—··—	Intermittent Stream
————	River/Creek
⌐ ⌐	Marsh/Swamp
▭	County and State Forest/Park
▭	National Forest/National Park
‿	Bridge
▲	Campground
⌒	Dam
•—•	Gate
❷	Information
℗	Parking
▲	Peak
🛆	Picnic Area
■	Point of Interest/Other Trailhead
❻	Trailhead
∥	Waterfall
❧	Viewpoint
N ⍟	True North (Magnetic North is approximately 15.5° East)

Acknowledgments

I would like to thank my wife, Sarah, for her assistance in gathering information for this guide and accompanying me while conducting field research. I also would like to acknowledge the help of my daughters, Claire amd Hannah, who endured (and enjoyed) many of these hikes, often in less than ideal weather conditions.

Introduction

Orange County is fortunate to have a large amount of open space and hiking opportunities. All the hikes listed are located in county, state, or federal open space; wilderness parks; or national forests. However, many of our open spaces remain threatened by development and toll road construction. Our county parks, state parks, and national forests are also threatened by declining budgets and skyrocketing visitation. Be aware of closures and use restrictions by visiting the agency Web sites listed for each hike.

Whether short and easy or a bit longer and more challenging, you'll enjoy each of these hikes much more if you wear good socks and appropriate footwear. Carry a comfortable day pack containing ample water, snacks and/or lunch, and extra clothing. Bring other items to increase your enjoyment of the hike, such as a camera; a manual to help identify plants, wildflowers, and birds; and binoculars.

Weather

Orange County generally enjoys a temperate climate. Even so, and depending on the season, the weather is subject to considerable extremes. Summer temperatures can exceed 100 degrees Fahrenheit. In the Santa Ana Mountains, winter storms can bring snow and freezing weather. It is important to be aware of the weather and prepare accordingly.

Familiarize yourself with the symptoms of both cold- and heat-related conditions, including hypothermia and particularly heat stroke. The best way to avoid these afflictions is to wear clothing appropriate to the weather conditions, drink plenty of fluids, eat enough, and maintain a pace that is within your physical limits.

Protect yourself from excessive exposure to sun by wearing a hat and using sunscreen. During summer, avoid hiking during the middle of the day. Early mornings are cooler, and birds and other wildlife are more active and more readily observed.

During winter, bring several layers of clothing. A water-proof shell is essential if rain is likely. Synthetic fabrics are often best for underlayers. Unlike cotton, synthetic fibers do not absorb lots of water and dry quickly. Add or subtract layers to prevent overheating or to keep warm. A warm hat or cap is particularly effective in conserving body heat.

Hiking Etiquette

Many of the trails described in this guide are multiuse trails that are open to equestrians, cyclists, runners, and hikers alike. A little courtesy goes a long way in ensuring everyone has an enjoyable experience. Horse riders should always be given the right of way. Large groups should yield to small groups or single users. Downhill traffic should yield to those coming uphill.

On wide trails and fire roads, always keep to the right, allowing others to pass on your left (just like in your car). Be aware of other users, and step to the right if you are being passed or stopping. Large groups should be particularly care-ful to not block the trails and should keep to the right and be aware of other users who may wish to pass.

Please stay on established trails. Cutting switchbacks causes erosion and damage to native plant species.

Trail Conditions

The trails described in this guide vary from well-maintained fire roads to steep, loose, and/or rutted footpaths. Trails are subject to erosion, mud- and rockslides, and washouts. In the state and county parks, trails may be closed for several days after heavy rains to prevent damage to the trail surface. Footwear should be appropriate to the trail conditions and caution exercised. You might want to check trail conditions before setting out for a hike by calling ahead or checking online.

Estimated Hiking Times

This guide provides an approximate time to complete each hike. This estimate is based upon an average speed of 2 miles per hour. You should add time if you are not a strong hiker or are traveling with small children. Subtract time if you are in good shape. Add time for picnics, rest stops, or other activities you plan for your outing.

Zero Impact

The trails that weave through Orange County parks and the Cleveland National Forest are heavily used and sometimes take a real beating. Because of their proximity to dense population, we, as trail users, must be especially vigilant to make sure our passing leaves no lasting mark. If we all leave our mark on the landscape, the parks and wildlands eventually will be despoiled.

These trails can accommodate plenty of human travel if everybody treats them with respect. However, even just a few thoughtless, badly mannered, or uninformed visitors can ruin them for everyone who follows.

Three Falcon Zero-Impact Principles

- Leave with everything you brought.
- Leave no sign of your visit.
- Leave the landscape as you found it.

Litter is the scourge of all trails. It is unsightly, polluting, and potentially dangerous to wildlife. Pack out all your own trash, including biodegradable items like orange peels, which might be sought out by area critters. You should also pack out garbage left trailside by less considerate hikers. Store a plastic bag in your pack to use for trash removal.

Don't approach or feed any wild creatures. The ground squirrel eyeing your snack food is best able to survive if it remains self-reliant—it is not likely to find cookies along the trail when winter comes.

Never pick flowers or gather plants or insects. So many people visit these trails that the cumulative effect of even small impacts can be huge.

Stay on established trails. Shortcutting and cutting switchbacks promotes erosion. Select durable surfaces, like rocks, logs, or sandy areas, for resting spots.

If possible, use outhouses at trailheads or along the trail. If outhouses are unavailable, pack in a lightweight trowel and a plastic bag so that you can bury your waste 6 to 8 inches deep. Pack out used toilet paper in a plastic bag. Make sure you relieve yourself at least 300 feet away from any surface water or boggy spot and off any established trail.

Remember to abide by the golden rule of backcountry travel: If you pack it in, pack it out! Keep your impact to a minimum; taking only pictures and leaving only footprints.

Consider giving something back to the parks and trails you enjoy by volunteering time to trail maintenance projects and supporting groups and organizations that help preserve and maintain parks and trails. Trails4All (13720 Florine Avenue, Paramount 90723; www.trails4all.org) is a nonprofit organization dedicated to preserving Orange County parks and maintaining its trails.

Put your ear to the ground and listen carefully. Thousands of people coming behind you are thankful for your courtesy and good sense.

Play It Safe

Generally hiking in Orange County is a safe and fun way to explore the outdoors. Though there are no guarantees, there is much you can do to help ensure each outing is safe and enjoyable. Below, you'll find an abbreviated list of hiking do's and don'ts, but by no means should this list be considered comprehensive. Verse yourself in the art of backcountry travel. You should also consider learning more about the flora, fauna, and geology of Southern California, which will greatly enhance your enjoyment and appreciation of these hikes. A good outdoor specialty store is a great place to begin.

Know the basics of first aid, including how to treat bleeding; bites and stings; and fractures, strains, or sprains. Few of the hikes are so remote that help can't be reached within a short time, but you would be wise to carry and know how to use simple supplies, such as over-the-counter pain relievers, bandages, and ointments. Pack a first-aid kit on each excursion.

The hills and mountains are home to a variety of wild-life, from squirrels to mountain lions. Squirrels can be host to disease, and mountain lions may attack if prompted by hunger. Rattlesnakes may be found on any of the hikes described, particularly from early spring to mid-fall. Watch where you put your hands and feet. If given a chance, most rattlesnakes will try to avoid a confrontation.

Poison oak is common throughout Orange County's hills, valleys, and mountains. Know how to identify this distinctive three-leaved plant and avoid all contact. Even the bare branches should be avoided.

Ticks are another pest to be avoided. They hang in the brush, waiting to drop on warm-blooded animals (people included), and some can carry Lyme disease. Check for ticks, and remove any before they have a chance to bite.

Most free-flowing water should be considered unsafe to drink if untreated. Bring all the water you need with you.

How to Use This Guide

The at-a-glance information at the beginning of each hike includes a short description, the hike distance in miles and type of trail (loop, out and back, or lollipop), the time required for an average hiker, difficulty (easy or moderate), elevation gain, the trail surface, the best season for hiking the trail, other trail users, whether dogs are allowed on the hike, applicable fees or permits, park/trail schedule, maps, and trail contacts for additional information. Directions to the trailhead are also provided, along with a general description of what you'll see along the way. A detailed route finder sets forth mileages between significant landmarks along the trail.

Maps

Reference to the pertinent U.S. Geological Survey (USGS) 7.5-minute topographical map is provided for each hike. Other maps covering the hikes and areas described in this guide are available through the USDA Forest Service; the Orange County Harbors, Beaches, and Parks Department; and at the respective state parks. Many of these are available online and can be printed out ahead of time.

Ranking the Hikes

Although all the hikes in this book are relatively easy, some are longer and have more elevation change than others. The following list ranks the hikes in each section of this book from easier to more challenging.

The Coast

Easier

1	Bolsa Chica Slough Trail
7	Valido Trail
4	Dilley Preserve Canyon–Mariposa Loop
5	Little Sycamore Canyon Trail
3	Laurel Canyon–Bommer Ridge Loop
2	East Cut-Across to Moro Ridge Loop
6	West Ridge, Lynx, and Cholla Trails

More Challenging

The Foothills

Easier

10	Santiago Creek Trail Loop
11	Peters Canyon Lake Loop
14	Riley Wilderness Park Loop
15	West Ridge and Oak Trail Loop
13	Live Oak Trail
8	Telegraph Canyon Trail via Rimcrest Entrance
9	Weir Canyon Trail Loop
12	Borrego Canyon to Red Rock Canyon

More Challenging

The Mountains

Easier

    23   El Cariso Nature Trail

    20   San Juan Loop Trail

    18   Holy Jim Trail

    19   Trabuco Trail

    21   Bear Canyon Trail

    24   Morgan Trail

    17   Santiago Trail

    16   Silverado Canyon–Silverado Motorway

    22   Los Pinos Peak

More Challenging

The Coast

The coastal areas of Orange County range from sandy beaches and tidal estuaries in the north to rocky shorelines and the rugged San Joaquin Hills in the south. Accordingly, the hiking experiences along Orange County's coast vary considerably. Bolsa Chica features an easy, wheelchair-accessible trail along a newly restored estuary that offers ample wildlife viewing and is perfect for a short family outing. Crystal Cove State Park, Laguna Coast Wilderness Park, and Aliso and Wood Canyons Wilderness Park offer longer and more challenging hikes into the coastal hills and canyons.

The coastal areas of Orange County are also some of the most threatened and biologically important in California. Estuaries and wetlands are probably the most ecologically diverse and fertile areas on the planet, but they are disappearing at an alarming rate. Most of these areas have fallen victim to housing developments or have been dredged to create marinas. Coastal hills, once covered in native coastal sage and other unique plant communities, are being graded to make way for toll roads and housing subdivisions, which are ubiquitous in southern Orange County. Still, Orange County has saved small remnants of this landscape. This guide will direct you to some of the most accessible and spectacular scenery remaining.

1 Bolsa Chica Slough Trail

This short hike makes a loop around this restored estuary and offers wonderful opportunities to observe a wide variety of bird species.

Distance: 1.5-mile loop
Approximate hiking time: 45 minutes
Difficulty: Easy; moderate for wheelchair access
Elevation gain: 15 feet
Trail surface: Wooden bridge, packed dirt
Best season: Year-round; winter months (November to March) offer the highest concentrations of migratory birds.
Other trail users: None
Canine compatibility: Dogs not permitted

Fees and permits: No fees or permits required
Schedule: Trail open sunrise to sunset; interpretive center open Tuesday through Friday 10:00 a.m. to 4:00 p.m.; Saturday 9:00 a.m. to noon; Sunday noon to 3:30 p.m.
Maps: USGS Seal Beach
Trail contacts: Bolsa Chica Conservancy, 3842 Warner Avenue, Huntington Beach 92469-4263; (714) 846-1114; www.bolsa chica.org

Finding the trailhead: Take either Warner Avenue or Golden West Street west from Interstate 405 (San Diego Freeway) to the Pacific Coast Highway (PCH/Highway 1). From Warner Avenue head about 1.5 miles south on the PCH. From Golden West Street drive north on the PCH for approximately 2.5 miles. Park in the small parking lot on the inland (east) side of the PCH. The lot is nearly opposite the entrance to Bolsa Chica State Beach.

The Hike

The Bolsa Chica Conservancy was formed in 1973 with an initial acquisition of 300 acres of wetlands next to the Pacific

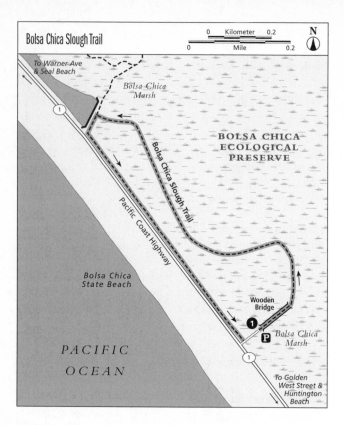

Coast Highway. Additions in 1997 and 2005 have brought that total to approximately 1,200 acres of prime marshland. In the summer 2006 engineering was completed that permitted seawater to flow into the reserve for the first time in more than one hundred years. This reserve, and the wetlands farther north in the Seal Beach National Wildlife Refuge, is one of the last remaining and most important fresh-saltwater estuaries in Southern California. Binoculars are a must, as you will have the opportunity to see a wide variety of birds, including terns, plovers, avocets, herons, egrets, various migratory sparrows, marsh hawks, and cormorants.

Begin the hike by taking the long wooden bridge over the shallow marshlands. On the opposite side of the bridge, at 0.1 mile, follow the dirt trail as it works its way to the left (north), then atop an old levee. Interpretive signs will help you identify wildlife.

The trail continues northward along levees on the inland side of the main, restored tidal marshlands. Note how different species of birds seek different types of food or use different search strategies. Beak size and shape play a role in their hunting techniques. Keep an eye out for nesting least terns on marsh islands and for sea sponges, jellyfish, and crabs in the shallow water.

At 0.8 mile you reach the northern apex of the trail and pass over an inlet for seawater into the marsh. Now you are heading south, the marsh on your left and the coastal highway and Pacific Ocean beyond to your right. As you head back south on the marsh's edge, take note of the small sand dunes—all that remains of a historically much more extensive dune system. Lilac-colored sea rocket and yellow beach primrose can be seen growing on these small dunes.

Depending on the time of year and time of day, the species and activity of the bird life will vary. Continue south along the marsh's edge until you return to the parking lot at 1.5 miles.

The interpretive center located on Warner Avenue, to the north of the parking area used for this hike, features exhibits, a saltwater aquarium, books, and docent-led tours. You can easily make a detour to the right and then head north from the dam crossing to reach the interpretive center.

Miles and Directions

0.0 Start from the parking lot and cross the long wooden bridge over the marsh.

0.1 The dirt trail begins on the far side of the bridge.

0.8 Reach the northern apex of the trail at the seawater inlet. (**Option:** To detour to the interpretive center, turn right here and then head left [north] on a marked trail.)

1.5 Arrive back at the parking lot.

2 East Cut-Across to Moro Ridge Loop

This longer loop hike takes you up one of the few unspoiled coastal canyons in the region and then up to a high ridge over the Pacific Ocean that offers great views of the rugged coastline.

Distance: 4.7-mile loop
Approximate hiking time: 2.5 hours
Difficulty: Moderate
Elevation gain: 750 feet
Trail surface: Fire road, some footpath
Best season: Fall through spring; early mornings in summer
Other trail users: Mountain bikers, equestrians, trail runners
Canine compatibility: Dogs not permitted

Fees and permits: $10 parking fee (Do not park at the elementary school—you will be towed.)
Schedule: Open 6:00 a.m. to sunset
Maps: USGS Laguna Beach
Trail contacts: Crystal Cove State Park, 8471 Pacific Coast Highway, Laguna Beach 92651; (949) 494-3539; www.crystal covestatepark.com

Finding the trailhead: Take Laguna Canyon Road (Highway 133) south from Interstate 5 (Santa Ana Freeway) or Interstate 405 (San Diego Freeway) to its terminus at the Pacific Coast Highway (PCH/ Highway 1). Drive north on the PCH for approximately 2.8 miles to El Moro Road, where you will find an elementary school and a traffic light. Turn right (east) onto El Moro Road and drive up the road to the entrance booth (a right-hand turn). Pay the parking fee here or at the self-serve machine in the parking area a short distance ahead. Currently the trailhead is at the west (bottom) end of this parking lot.

Note: The initial section of this trail (a fire road) eventually will be paved to provide access to a planned campground in the canyon bottom. Once this road is built, you should plan on parking in a day-

East Cut-Across to Moro Ridge Loop

No Name Ridge Trail

West Cut-Across

Moro Canyon Trail

CRYSTAL COVE STATE PARK

Poles Tr.

No Name Ridge Trail

East Cut-Across Trail

To Corona Del Mar

El Moro Road

School

Moro Creek

Moro Canyon Trail

Moro Ridge Trail

Pacific Coast Highway

BFI

Moro Ridge Trail

Emerald Vista

PACIFIC OCEAN

To Laguna Beach

use lot at the bottom of the new paved road and begin your hike from that point.

The Hike

This hike takes you in a loop from the lower portions of Moro Canyon, up to the high ridgeline on its southern edge, then back down to your starting point. A broad spectrum of terrain and habitat are explored without committing as much time as the longer hikes in Crystal Cove State Park typically require. In spring the canyon bottom flows with water and the hills are green with fresh growth and seasonal wildflowers. As you descend the high Moro Ridge, you will be rewarded with spectacular ocean vistas. You will also be afforded views south and east into the wild canyons and hills that are now part of Laguna Coast Wilderness Park and Irvine Open Space.

To begin the hike, take the fire road/trail that heads south from the vicinity of the entrance booth; the trail winds downhill into the bottom of Moro Canyon at 0.4 mile.

This section of fire road is set to be paved for access to the campground in the canyon bottom. Once construction is completed, you can drive down and begin your hike from a day-use lot at the bottom of the road adjacent to the campground. Follow the Moro Canyon Trail (wide fire road) east up the canyon. Observe the open coastal sage scrub and grass hillsides once common throughout Southern California. After a stream crossing, the trail climbs up onto the left (north) side of the creek. At 1.5 miles you will come to the intersection with the East Cut-Across Trail, which is on your right (south).

Turn right, cross the creek, and follow the East Cut-Across Trail for 1.0 mile as it winds up the canyon wall. At 2.5 miles you will reach the intersection with the Moro Ridge Trail. Head right (west) on the Moro Ridge Trail as it gently descends along the ridgetop. Just before the trail begins a steep descent at 3.2 miles, a left-hand fork leads to the Emerald Vista. A detour to the Emerald Vista will add about 0.5 mile to your hike.

Continue down the Moro Ridge Trail until you are near the Pacific Coast Highway and the route becomes paved. Here, at 4.0 miles, turn right onto the BFI footpath that heads down to the bottom of Moro Canyon. Once you reach the floor of the canyon at 4.3 miles, turn left and return to the parking lot.

Miles and Directions

0.0   Start at the trailhead near the entrance booth and head south on the fire road/trail.

0.4   The trail comes to the bottom of Moro Canyon.

1.5   Turn right at the junction onto the East Cut-Across Trail.

2.5   The trail reaches the ridgetop and the Moro Ridge Trail; turn right.

3.2   Pass the Emerald Vista Trail junction. (**Option:** Follow the path to Emerald Vista for an additional 0.5-mile round-trip.)

4.0   The footpath leads right (north) down to Moro Canyon.

4.3   Reach the bottom of Moro Canyon. Turn left to return to the trailhead and parking area.

4.7   Arrive back at the parking area.

3 Laurel Canyon–Bommer Ridge Loop

This hike begins with a scenic footpath that proceeds up an open valley into a riparian canyon featuring several seasonal stream crossings and the 50-foot Laurel Canyon Falls. Fire roads then lead to an ocean overlook and an easy downhill back to your car.

Distance: 3.5-mile loop
Approximate hiking time: 1.75 hours
Difficulty: Moderate
Elevation gain: 665 feet
Trail surface: Footpath through Laurel Canyon; fire road on Bommer Ridge and Willow Canyon Trails
Best season: Fall through spring; early mornings in summer
Other trail users: Hikers only in Laurel Canyon; mountain bikers and equestrians on Bommer

Ridge and Willow Canyon Trails
Canine compatibility: Dogs not permitted
Fees and permits: $3 parking fee
Schedule: Park open 7:00 a.m. to sunset daily; parking lot open 8:00 a.m. to 4:00 p.m.
Maps: USGS Laguna Beach
Trail contacts: Laguna Coast Wilderness Park, Nix Center at Little Sycamore Canyon, 18751 Laguna Canyon Road, Laguna Beach 92651; (949) 923-2235; www.ocparks.com

Finding the trailhead: From Interstate 5 (Santa Ana Freeway) or Interstate 405 (San Diego Freeway), take Laguna Canyon Road (Highway 133) southwest to a point just south of the intersection with El Toro Road. The park entrance is located on the right (west). The small gravel lot fills early on nice weekend days.

The Hike

This is one of the best hikes in Orange County and perfectly suited to a family outing. Although park volunteers often

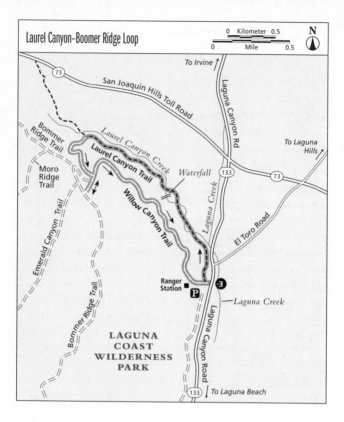

Laurel Canyon-Boomer Ridge Loop

0   Kilometer   0.5

0   Mile   0.5

N

To Irvine

San Joaquin Hills Toll Road

Laguna Canyon Rd

73

Bommer Ridge Trail

Laurel Canyon Creek

To Laguna Hills

Laurel Canyon Trail

Moro Ridge Trail

Waterfall

133

73

Emerald Canyon Trail

Willow Canyon Trail

Laguna Creek

El Toro Road

Bommer Ridge Trail

Ranger Station

P

3

Laguna Creek

LAGUNA COAST WILDERNESS PARK

Laguna Canyon Road

133   To Laguna Beach

recommend doing this hike in the reverse order as described here, don't fall for it. Save the long, exposed Willow Canyon fire road for your return stretch. Also, if you do not feel like completing the entire hike (e.g., the kids rebel), you can still enjoy the quiet and shady scenery of Laurel Canyon and simply retrace your steps back to your start point.

As you work your way up the secluded recesses of Laurel Canyon, you will have a chance to view scenery seen by few people. You'll also see a large number of native plants, birds of prey, and migratory songbirds, as well as a variety of wildflowers in winter and spring. The only sad note to this hike is the intrusion of the San Joaquin Hills Toll Road through the upper reaches of the canyon.

From the parking area walk a short distance west on the road toward the ranger station. Before beginning your hike, be sure to sign in at the volunteer desk located adjacent to the trailhead. The signed trail begins as a footpath heading northeast through sandstone boulders. The trail then turns north, climbing up and over a small ridge into the open area of Laurel Canyon. Head up the footpath into the mouth of the canyon, passing old orchards and large sandstone out-crops at 0.3 mile.

The trail enters the mouth of the canyon proper and becomes shaded by old sycamore and oak. At 0.5 mile you make the first of three crossings of the seasonal Laurel Canyon Creek. At the second stream crossing, if you look carefully you might see seashell fossils embedded in the sandstone boulders in the creek, testament to this area once having been seabed.

The trail begins to climb along the right side of the canyon, making a final steep climb until at 0.8 mile you reach a level spot and a last stream crossing. At this point you are atop 50-foot-high Laurel Canyon Falls. Use care when approaching the edge of the falls, particularly if water is present on the slippery rocks.

Now the trail wanders along the left side of the stream under ancient oak and sycamore trees. The canyon again widens and the footpath eventually passes a wooden gate and joins a narrow fire road at 1.5 miles. Turn left (south-west) and follow the trail as it climbs steeply upward out of the canyon to the Willow Canyon Trail junction. Head right (northwest) from the junction, stay left at the next junction, and continue a few hundred yards to the ridgeline at 2.0 miles. Here you can enjoy views west to the Pacific Ocean and into Emerald Canyon.

Retrace your route downhill, but continue past the junction with the trail leading into Laurel Canyon. Instead continue downhill on the wide Willow Canyon fire road, which passes high above the southern side of Laurel Canyon. This trail leads you back to the ranger station and your car.

Miles and Directions

0.0 Start at the signed footpath near the ranger station.

0.3 Pass sandstone outcrops.

0.5 Make the first stream crossing.

0.8 Make the final stream crossing and reach the top of Laurel Canyon Falls.

1.5 Join the fire road and head left (southwest).

1.8+ Reach the junction with Willow Canyon Trail.

2.0 Reach the crest of the ridge and Bommer Ridge fire road and take in the views. Retrace your steps, bypassing the Laurel Canyon Trail and continuing downhill on the Willow Canyon fire road.

3.5 Arrive back at the ranger station and parking area.

4 Dilley Preserve Canyon-Mariposa Loop

This excellent short loop follows a footpath up an open canyon populated with sycamore and oak until you climb atop a high ridge. From here you follow a scenic foot trail down the spine of another ridge to your starting point.

Distance: 1.8-mile loop
Approximate hiking time: 1 hour
Difficulty: Moderate
Elevation gain: 310 feet
Trail surface: Foot trail, rocky in sections
Best season: Fall through spring; early mornings in summer
Other trail users: None
Canine compatibility: Dogs not permitted
Fees and permits: $3 parking

fee (cash in envelope)
Schedule: Park open 7:00 a.m. to sunset daily; parking lot open 8:00 a.m. to 4:00 p.m.
Maps: USGS Laguna Beach
Trail contacts: Laguna Coast Wilderness Park, Nix Center at Little Sycamore Canyon, 18751 Laguna Canyon Road, Laguna Beach 92651; (949) 923-2235; www.ocparks.com

Finding the trailhead: The parking area for the James Dilley Preserve is located on the east side of Laguna Canyon Road (Highway 133), a little more than 0.1 mile north of the San Joaquin Hills Toll Road (Highway 73) and 0.9 mile north of El Toro Road.

From Interstate 5 (Santa Ana Freeway) or Interstate 405 (San Diego Freeway), take Laguna Canyon Road (Highway 133) southwest to a signal just north of the San Joaquin Hill Toll Road. Make a U-turn here and head north. Turn right into the small dirt parking area is located immediately east of Highway 133. Use the self-pay envelopes for the $3 parking fee. The trail begins at the northeast end of the parking area.

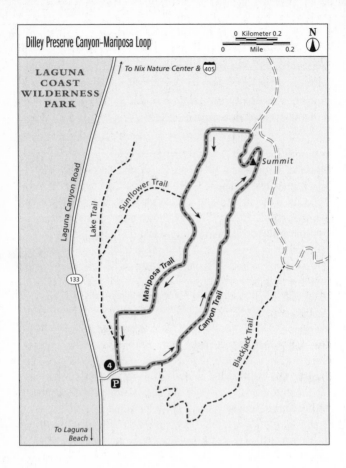

Dilley Preserve Canyon-Mariposa Loop

0 Kilometer 0.2
0 Mile 0.2

N

LAGUNA
COAST
WILDERNESS
PARK

To Nix Nature Center & 405

Summit

Laguna Canyon Road

Sunflower Trail

Lake Trail

Mariposa Trail

Canyon Trail

Blackjack Trail

133

4

P

To Laguna
Beach

The Hike

Starting at the covered picnic area and information kiosk in
the Dilley Reserve parking area, head east on the Canyon
Trail (Signpost 55). As the name suggests, the Canyon Trail

heads up a scenic open canyon that's generously populated with sycamore and ancient live oak. The Canyon Trail begins as a wide doubletrack and soon passes a grove of large sycamores. After a short distance the trail becomes a nice footpath and crosses a small footbridge.

Stay left at all trail junctions, including the junction with the Blackjack Trail. As the trail gently ascends the canyon, you pass groves of sycamore trees and the traffic noise of busy Laguna Canyon Road is soon muted by the sounds of scrub jays and migratory birds. The only sign of civilization are power lines on the ridge. The path is alternatively shaded and sunny as it works its way up the canyon, passing through laurel sumac and other thick coastal scrub.

Where the canyon steepens, the trail switchbacks to the left to where you climb out of the canyon on a rocky ridge. Atop this final climb, after 1.0 mile of hiking, you arrive at a large open area (where an underground storage tank is buried) and the end of the Canyon Trail at an elevation of about 625 feet. Enjoy the unobstructed 360-degree vistas, which provide a bird's-eye view of the entire Laguna Canyon area and views of the Santa Ana Mountains to the east.

From the top of the Canyon Trail, head directly left and across the open area to where you will see a signpost (#56) for the Mariposa Trail (a footpath), which snakes west and south across and down the spine of a scenic chaparral-covered ridge. The trail alternates between smooth trail, sandstone steps, and loose cobbles. The sandstone and cobbles attest to this area once having been part of a shallow seabed. In the nearby hills, fossilized whale bones and marine creatures have been unearthed by residential development.

At a bit more than 1.3 miles, a signpost at the fork marks the Sunflower Trail's divergence off to the right and down another, rockier ridge. Continue straight (the left-hand fork) and continue down the Mariposa Trail as it follows the main ridgeline.

Near the bottom of the ridge, make sure to stay atop the crest of the ridge, avoiding any apparent trails heading off the main track. A short rise and final descent bring you to the canyon floor at 1.6 miles. Here the Mariposa Trail dead-ends into the Lake Trail. Turn left (south) onto the Lake Trail and follow it back to your starting point.

Miles and Directions

- **0.0** Start at Signpost 55 and head east on the Canyon Trail.
- **0.5** Pass groves of sycamore and ancient oak.
- **0.8** Switchback up the ridge to the left.
- **1.0** Arrive at the summit, an open area atop a buried water tank. Head left across the open area to the start of Mariposa Trail (Signpost 56). Hike along and down the spine of the ridge on a nice footpath.
- **1.3** Reach the junction with the Sunflower Trail. Stay left (straight) at the fork and follow the Mariposa Trail down the ridge.
- **1.6** At bottom of the ridge, intersect the Lake Trail. Turn left onto the Lake Trail.
- **1.8** The Lake Trail ends at the parking area.

5 Little Sycamore Canyon Trail

This short in-and-out hike quickly gains elevation then takes you into the remarkably remote-feeling upper Little Sycamore Canyon. A casual stroll in the upper canyon leads to a final uphill push to reach a high point with nice views. This is an excellent family hike. An optional (and much longer) loop hike is also possible.

Distance: 2.0 miles out and back; 5.2-mile loop option

Approximate hiking time: 1 hour

Difficulty: Moderate

Elevation gain: 370 feet; 803 feet for loop option

Trail surface: Fire road, foot trail; steep and rocky in sections

Best season: Fall through spring; early morning in summer

Other trail users: None

Canine compatibility: Dogs not permitted

Fees and permits: $3 parking fee (cash in envelope)

Schedule: Park open 7:00 a.m. to sunset daily; parking lot open 8:00 a.m. to 4:00 p.m.

Maps: USGS Laguna Beach

Trail contacts: Laguna Coast Wilderness Park, Nix Center at Little Sycamore Canyon, 18751 Laguna Canyon Road, Laguna Beach 92651; (949) 923-2235; www.ocparks.com

Finding the trailhead: This hike begins from the Laguna Coast Wilderness Park's signature Nix Nature Center. To reach the center, take Laguna Canyon Road (Highway 133) south for about 2.8 miles from Highway 405 to the exit for the Nix Nature Center. The exit is located 1.7 miles north on Highway 133 from El Toro Road (1 mile north of Highway 73). Adjacent to the Nix Center are a large parking lot and picnic areas under a grove of sycamores. Park here and pay the $3 fee (machine takes $1 bills or quarters only).

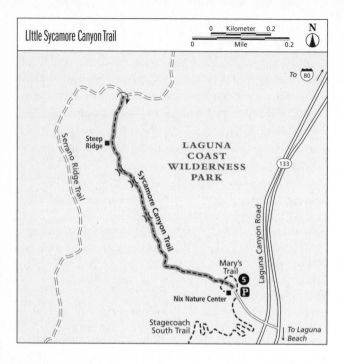

0 Kilometer 0.2
0 Mile 0.2

N

To (80)

Serrano Ridge Trail

Steep
Ridge

LAGUNA
COAST
WILDERNESS
PARK

Sycamore Canyon Trail

(133)

Laguna Canyon Road

Mary's
Trail

5

P

Nix Nature Center

Stagecoach
South Trail

To Laguna
Beach

The Hike

Either before or after your hike, be sure to visit the Nix Nature Center, which contains great exhibits and activities for children and adults alike. There are toilets and water fountains at the center.

From the west end of the parking lot, head directly west up a small hill on the wide Little Sycamore Canyon Trail. (If you visit the nature center first, you can head northwest from the center's entrance along Mary's Trail, cross a bridge, and make a quick switchback to the Little Sycamore Canyon Trail.)

Almost immediately, the Little Sycamore Canyon Trail begins a steep climb directly up the hillside. A short bit of flat leads to more steep uphill hiking, made more difficult by loose cobbles on the wide trail. Many a would-be hiker is turned back by this initial section of the trail—but persevere. After about only 0.1 mile, the trail mostly levels and begins a winding traverse to the northwest along the side of the hill. Scrub oak, laurel sumac, and toyon (with its characteristic red berries) line the trail.

At the 0.4-mile mark, you reach a large open and flat area. At this point you can look east down into rugged Little Sycamore Canyon, descending back to the Nix Center. To the northeast are steep sandstone outcrops hidden from Laguna Canyon; to the north and northwest lies the open watershed that drains into Little Sycamore Canyon. From here the trail descends a bit, becoming a well-groomed footpath, and crosses the first of three small footbridges.

The trail winds its way through dense chaparral and enters a valley that is shielded from the noise and development visible from Laguna Canyon Road. The journey becomes suddenly quiet and serene, with the path ahead only gently gaining elevation. Along the way, you cross two more footbridges.

After the last footbridge (0.75 mile), the trail begins another steep climb up a ridge. This section of the trail features excellent views in all directions, as well as many large and small loose cobbles in the trail. About halfway up the ridge, the going eases considerably. You can coax small children up to this point—a small scrub oak visible on the ridge ahead—with promises of a section of level hiking just beyond. A last small uphill stretch brings you to a fire road, the Serrano Ridge Trail, at 1.0 mile.

Take a good breather and enjoy a picnic or snack. It's an easy downhill trek back to the Nix Center and your car.

Loop Option
If the short jaunt up Little Sycamore Canyon Trail to Serrano Ridge was not enough for you, you can continue from this point and enjoy a wonderful 5.2-mile (total) loop hike back to the Nix Center. The extended journey lies on a very scenic fire road and singletrack shared with mountain bikers.

From the junction of Little Sycamore Canyon and Serrano Ridge Trails, turn left (west) onto the Serrano Ridge Trail fire road. This trail winds its way west and then south along the ridgetop, with a number of short climbs and descents along the way. After following Serrano Ridge for almost 1.5 miles, you descend to a flat and a four-way intersection at 2.5 miles. Turn left (east) onto the Camarillo Canyon fire road. The trail quickly descends the hill, reaching a shady area under large oaks in Camarillo Canyon at 2.8 miles. Continue east down Camarillo Canyon for about 0.5 mile to a gate (3.3 miles). Just beyond the gate, turn left and head uphill on Stagecoach South Trail—a great singletrack. Follow this trail as it winds its way up the hill and then back down to the Nix Center parking area.

Miles and Directions

- **0.0** Start at the parking area and head west up the Little Sycamore Canyon Trail on a steep initial incline.
- **0.1+** The trail levels and traverses to the northwest along the hillside.
- **0.4** Reach an open level area above the rugged lower section of Little Sycamore Canyon.

0.75 Cross the last footbridge and begin climbing steeply up the ridge.

1.0 Reach Serrano Ridge Trail fire road and your turnaround point.

2.0 Arrive back at the parking area and Nix Nature Center.

6 West Ridge, Lynx, and Cholla Trails

This scenic hike descends the long, scenic ridge that separates Laguna and Woods Canyons. At the end of the ridge, you take a short loop hike into Woods Canyon before returning to the ridge trail and then back to your staring point.

Distance: 4.7-mile lollipop
Approximate hiking time: 2.5 hours
Difficulty: Moderate
Elevation gain: 820 feet
Trail surface: Fire road, foot trail; steep and rocky in sections
Best season: Fall through spring; early mornings in summer
Other trail users: Mountain bikers, equestrians, trail runners
Canine compatibility: Dogs not permitted

Fees and permits: No fees or permits required
Schedule: Open sunrise to sunset daily
Maps: USGS Laguna Beach, San Juan Capistrano
Trail contacts: Aliso and Wood Canyons Wilderness Park, 28373 Alicia Parkway, Laguna Niguel 92677; (949) 923-2200; www .ocparks.com/alisoandwood canyons

Finding the trailhead: From Interstate 5 (Santa Ana Freeway) or Interstate 405 (San Diego Freeway), take Laguna Canyon Road (Highway 133) southwest to Forest Avenue/Third Street. Take Third Street up the short, very steep hill. At the stop sign turn left onto Park Avenue and follow Park Avenue uphill to its end at Alta Laguna

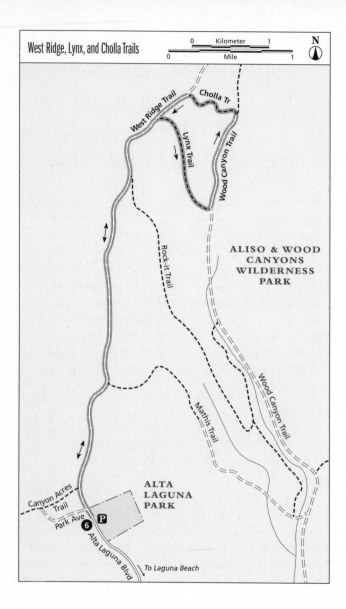

Kilometer

Mile

N

West Ridge Trail

Cholla Tr

Lynx Trail

Wood Canyon Trail

ALISO & WOOD
CANYONS
WILDERNESS
PARK

Rock-it Trail

Wood Canyon Trail

Mathis Trail

ALTA
LAGUNA
PARK

Canyon Acres
Trail

Park Ave

6 P

Alta Laguna Blvd

To Laguna Beach

Boulevard. Turn left (north) onto Alta Laguna and go 0.2 mile to the parking area at Alta Laguna Park. The trail begins at the northwest corner of the parking area.

The Hike

This hike has it all, including vistas of the Pacific Ocean from the heights above Laguna Beach and a visit to the depths of a coastal canyon shaded by ancient oaks and sycamores. Starting atop Alta Laguna Boulevard, you descend to the north along the West Ridge Trail as it undulates along the ridge separating busy Laguna Canyon from the quiet solitude of Wood Canyon.

Eventually the footpath takes you from the ridge into the upper reaches of Wood Canyon. Water flows in Wood Canyon Creek during much of the year, and the careful observer will be rewarded with glimpses of wildlife. Returning to the West Ridge Trail via the Cholla Trail, you complete a loop and explore a variety of terrain.

From the parking area head northwest on a path that soon joins the wide West Ridge Trail at the highest spot in Aliso and Wood Canyons Wilderness Park. Head north on the trail, which soon begins a long descent and then curves up slightly to the right (southeast). Stay left (north) at the junction with the Mathis Trail at 0.5 mile.

Another descent and a few small rises bring you to a junction with the Rock-it Trail near a water tank at 1.5 miles; stay left (north) here. Continue along the West Ridge Trail; a final descent brings you to a gate and another trail junction at 2.0 miles. Head right on the Lynx Trail, a wide footpath that rapidly descends the side of a sage scrub–covered ridge to the tree-shaded bottom of Wood Canyon at 2.6 miles.

The Lynx Trail deposits you on the wide Wood Canyon Trail amid large oaks and next to Wood Canyon Creek. Head left (north) up the Wood Canyon Trail until you reach an open area just before a park gate. At 2.8 miles, from the left (northwest) side of the open area, proceed up the Cholla Trail. This footpath climbs back up to meet the West Ridge Trail at 3.2 miles. Turn left (southwest) on the West Ridge Trail and soon pass the Lynx Trail junction.

Continue the way you came, climbing steadily back to your car and starting point.

Miles and Directions

0.0 Start on the path at the northwest corner of the parking lot.

0.6 Reach the junction with the Mathis Trail; stay left (north).

1.5 Arrive at the Rock-it Trail junction; stay left (north).

2.0 Turn right (east) onto the Lynx Trail.

2.6 Reach the bottom of the canyon and turn left (north).

2.8 Turn left (northwest) at the Cholla Trail junction.

3.2 Rejoin the West Ridge Trail.

4.7 Arrive back at the parking area.

7 Valido Trail

Looking for a short, family-oriented hike that leads to a stunning ocean vista? This hike may be for you. Although the Valido Trail makes a significant climb from a residential area in South Laguna, the trail is short enough that even small children can be coaxed along.

Distance: 1.1 miles out and back
Approximate hiking time: 1 hour
Difficulty: Easy to moderate
Elevation gain: 400 feet
Trail surface: Foot trail; steep in sections
Best season: Fall through spring; early mornings in summer
Other trail users: None
Canine compatibility: Dogs not permitted

Fees and permits: No fees or permits required
Schedule: Open sunrise to sunset daily
Maps: USGS San Juan Capistrano
Trail contacts: Aliso and Wood Canyons Wilderness Park, 28373 Alicia Parkway, Laguna Niguel 92677; (949) 923-2200; www .ocparks.com

Finding the trailhead: From Interstate 5 (Santa Ana Freeway) or Interstate 405 (San Diego Freeway), take Laguna Canyon Road (Highway 133) southwest to the Pacific Coast Highway (PCH/Highway 1). Head left (south) on the PCH for about 3.5 miles to West Street in South Laguna. Turn left (east) onto West Street; go less than 0.2 mile and turn left (north) onto Valido Drive. As you round the curve, the trailhead is on your left (north). Park on the street, but avoid blocking any residential access.

The Hike

From the gate at the trailhead, head up the canyon on the wide Valido Trail until a sign marks the point where the

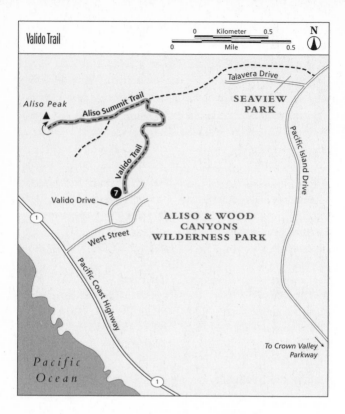

trail becomes a footpath. The trail proceeds along a small creek for a short distance before making a steep climb up a hillside. Log steps and switchbacks make the short but steep ascent fairly straightforward. At the second switchback you can gaze west to the Pacific Ocean and east up the narrow Valido Canyon.

Though the wild upper Valido Canyon is somewhat marred by development atop the ridge, the trail heads through largely unspoiled open space and dense coastal chaparral.

As you continue up to the steep footpath to the ridge, the grade slackens and the trail soon reaches the ridge and intersects the wide Aliso Summit Trail. Turn left (west) onto the Aliso Summit Trail and go straight (west), eventually making a short but steep climb up to the summit of Aliso Peak.

The hike finishes atop Aliso Peak's rounded summit, which seemingly hangs above Aliso Creek and the Pacific Ocean. The surrounding terrain is precipitously steep in places, so it is important that you don't wander off the established trails. Atop the summit, you are rewarded with spectacular views west to the Pacific Ocean and northeast up Aliso Canyon into the heart of Aliso and Wood Canyons Wilderness Park.

This is the turnaround point. Take time to enjoy the view before heading back to your car on the same path.

Miles and Directions

0.0 Start at the trailhead gate and head upcanyon.

0.1+ Cross Valido Canyon Creek and begin a steep uphill climb.

0.4 Reach a ridge and the Aliso Summit Trail. Head left (west).

0.55 Reach the crest of Aliso Peak and your turnaround point.

1.1 Arrive back at the trailhead.

The Foothills

The foothills of Orange County provide a wide diversity of geography and wildlife. For many years much of the open space in Orange County's foothills has been closed to public access, with cattle grazing and agriculture the prevalent land uses. Although large landowners and their representatives on the Orange County Board of Supervisors have pushed hard for development of most of rural Orange County, notable efforts have been made to preserve a portion of these unique and valuable habitats.

A number of open space, state, and county parks have saved pieces of this landscape from the blade of the developer's bulldozer, although more land remains threatened, especially by the construction of new toll roads through state and county parklands. Canyons, grasslands, lakes, seasonal streams, and hilltops are all found here. The hikes in this section range from short strolls along strips of open space near developments to more remote locales where you can almost imagine the Orange County of fifty or even one hundred years.

8 Telegraph Canyon Trail via Rimcrest Entrance

This hike descends directly into the heart of Telegraph Canyon and Chino Hills State Park. You then hike up the wide Telegraph Canyon Trail to a nice shaded picnic area. This hike allows you to quickly access a part of Chino Hills that seems far away from civilization.

Distance: 4.8 miles out and back
Approximate hiking time: 2.5 hours
Difficulty: Moderate
Elevation gain: 525 feet
Trail surface: Foot trail, fire road
Best season: Fall through spring; early mornings in summer
Other trail users: Mountain bikers, equestrians, trail runners
Canine compatibility: Dogs not permitted
Fees and permits: No fees or permits required
Schedule: Open 8:00 a.m. to sunset daily
Maps: USGS Yorba Linda, Prado Dam
Trail contacts: Chino Hills State Park, 1879 Jackson Street, Riverside 92504; (951) 780-6222; www.parks.ca.gov

Finding the trailhead: Take Highway 91 (Riverside Freeway) east to Imperial Highway (Highway 90) and head north. Follow Imperial Highway to Yorba Linda Boulevard and turn east (right). At Fairmont Boulevard turn left (north). After 1.8 miles turn left onto Rimcrest Street. Park on the right-hand side of Rimcrest Street near Blue Gum. Parking is permitted from 8:00 a.m. until dark. The trailhead lies straight ahead at the end of Rimcrest Street.

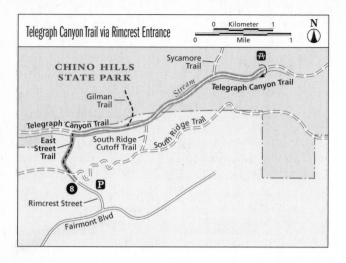

The Hike

Note: In fall 2008 a devastating fire swept through the entirety of Chino Hills State Park. At this writing, this and all other park trails are closed. The park should reopen in 2009 and over time the devastation be healed by Mother Nature.

Chino Hills State Park is a huge, natural open-space area in the hills north of Santa Ana Canyon. The area serves as a critical link in a biological corridor that connects the Santa Ana Mountains with the Whittier Hills. Its rolling, grassy hills and sycamore and oak–filled canyons are vast and unspoiled.

This hike takes you into the depths of Telegraph Canyon, which runs eastward from its mouth at the Carbon Canyon up toward one of Chino Hills' highest points, San Juan Peak. Starting from the park's Rimcrest entrance, you are plunged immediately into the upper reaches of Tele-graph Canyon.

The hike begins by passing the metal gate at the park entrance and proceeding more or less due north on the Easy Street Trail, across the fire road (South Ridge Trail). The trail begins a descent into a narrow side canyon, staying on the canyon's left side. You cross a creek and find yourself on the wide Telegraph Canyon Trail at 0.4 mile. Note this trail junction for your return.

You are now in the depths of Telegraph Canyon. Turn right (east) and proceed up the trail along the canyon bot-tom. After the occasional seasonal stream crossing, you will see trails that head both left and right up side canyons and hillsides. Don't stray from the canyon bottom. As you head up Telegraph Canyon, you'll encounter a rich riparian habitat.

Telegraph Canyon Trail begins to pass under an increas-ing number of sycamores and oaks as it parallels the stream. The Little Canyon Trail heads off right (south) at 1.2 miles; continue straight. The grade increases slightly, and the Syca-more Trail heads off to the left (north). Again, stay on the main trail along the canyon bottom.

You soon reach a nicely shaded section of trail, with a beautiful clearing on the right (south). A picnic table under the oaks at 2.4 miles is a perfect place for lunch or a snack. The surrounding hills hide all evidence of human develop-ment, providing a sense of remoteness seldom encountered in congested Orange County. In winter the emerald-green hillsides and free-flowing creek are delightful.

After resting and relaxing, simply return the way you came, making sure to take the Easy Street Trail on your left back up to the Rimcrest entrance and your car.

If you head left out of Telegraph Canyon too early by taking the Little Canyon Trail, you will intersect the South Ridge Trail. You can turn right (west) onto this trail to get back to the Rimcrest entrance.

Miles and Directions

0.0 Start at the trailhead at the end of Rimcrest Street and pass the metal gate. Cross the South Ridge Trail fire road and head north down the Easy Street Trail footpath.

0.4 Reach the bottom of the Easy Street Trail and intersect the Telegraph Canyon Trail (fire road); turn right (east) onto the Telegraph Canyon Trail.

1.0 The Gilman Trail intersects from the left; stay on the Telegraph Canyon Trail.

1.1 The South Ridge Cutoff Trial heads off to the right; stay on the main trail.

1.2 The Little Canyon Trail intersects from the right (south); continue straight.

1.9 The Sycamore Trail heads off to the left (north); stay on the main trail along the canyon bottom.

2.4 Arrive at the shaded picnic area. Head back down the Telegraph Canyon Trail.

4.4 Turn left at the East Street Trail.

4.8 Arrive back at the Rimcrest entrance and your car.

9 Weir Canyon Trail Loop

This great loop hike on publicly owned land is suitable for the entire family. Although adjacent to newer development, you are afforded great views to the east into the greater Weir Canyon Wilderness Area (managed by the Irvine Ranch Conservancy) and the Santa Ana Mountain Range.

Distance: 4.0-mile loop
Approximate hiking time: 2 hours
Difficulty: Easy
Elevation gain: 600 feet
Trail surface: Footpath, fire road
Best season: Fall through spring; early mornings in summer
Other trail users: Mountain bikers, equestrians
Canine compatibility: Dogs not permitted
Fees and permits: No fees or permits required
Schedule: Open 7:00 a.m. to sunset daily
Maps: USGS Black Star Canyon
Trail contacts: Weir Canyon Wilderness Park, Irvine Ranch Conservancy, Portola Field Office, 4727 Portola Parkway, Irvine 92602; (714) 508-4757; Weir Canyon Wilderness Area: www .irvineranchwildlands.org/land/ weir.asp#

Finding the trailhead: Take Highway 91 (Riverside Freeway) east to the Weir Canyon exit and head south. Turn right (west) onto Serrano Avenue. Follow Serrano Avenue until you reach Hidden Canyon Road. Turn left (south) onto Hidden Canyon Road and follow it until you reach the dead end at Overlook Terrace. Park at the corner by the barrier. Do *not* park in the residential areas or along Avenida de Santiago.

The Hike

This small part of Weir Canyon is part of the as of yet unofficial Orange County Weir Canyon Wilderness Park—a

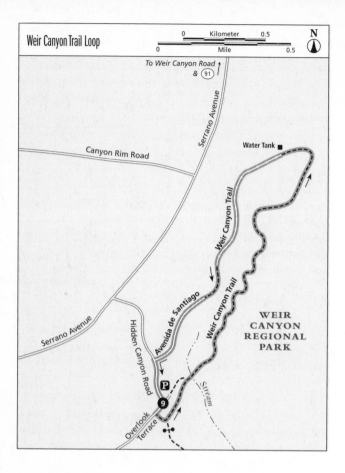

small jewel amidst the increased development of the Anaheim Hills region. The park and this hike lie adjacent to the larger Weir Canyon Wilderness Area, which is managed by the Irvine Ranch Conservancy. The conservancy offers longer docent-led hikes into the greater Weir Canyon.

As you follow the trail, you are afforded excellent views eastward into serene valleys and rugged foothills and toward the higher reaches of the Santa Ana Mountains. The trail winds in and out of small side canyons on the western edge of Weir Canyon.

From the trailhead take the wide trail/fire road directly east and slightly downhill. At 0.1 mile you will come to a gate. Turn left and head uphill on an unmarked but obvious foot trail.

The path gradually rises and levels, with scenic overlooks into Weir Canyon on your right (southeast) and sandstone outcrops to your left (northwest). At an open spot at 0.3 mile, just before the trail descends under oaks, a trail intersects from the left. Stay right, descending to a seasonal stream crossing at 0.4 mile.

From the stream the trail alternately climbs and descends as it winds in and out of small side canyons. Pass a small gray sandstone bluff directly above the trail, which then heads slightly west, passing over a ridge.

The trail continues along the upper reaches of Weir Canyon, bordering a residential development at 2.5 miles. At this point the trail begins to head in a southerly direction, passing a large water tank. Follow the trail along the ridge and then down to the Avenida de Santiago cul-de-sac at 3.5 miles. An easy downhill walk on Avenida de Santiago, then a left onto Hidden Canyon Road, leads back to your car at 3.8 miles.

Miles and Directions

0.0 Start at the barrier on Overlook Terrace.

0.1 Turn left at the gate, following the footpath.

0.3 Another path joins from the left; stay right (northeast).

0.4 Cross the small stream.

2.5 The trail curves left next to a housing development.

3.5 Reach the cul-de-sac; head down Avenida de Santiago.

3.8 Turn left (south) onto Hidden Canyon Road and arrive back at your car.

10 Santiago Creek Trail Loop

This easy, meandering hike follows a series of footpaths along and across the lower Santiago Creek. Santiago Creek is one of the main drainages for the Santa Ana Mountains. A great outing for families, the hike features sycamore and oak trees, picnic areas, and historical ties to early Orange County history.

Distance: 2.2-mile loop

Approximate hiking time: 1 hour

Difficulty: Easy

Elevation gain: 100 feet

Trail surface: Footpaths

Best season: Fall through spring; early mornings in summer

Other trail users: None

Canine compatibility: Dogs permitted

Fees and permits: $3 parking—either quarters or very crisp dollar bills

Schedule: Park open 7:00 a.m. to sunset daily; parking lot open 8:00 a.m. to 4:00 p.m.

Maps: USGS Orange

Trail contacts: Santiago Oaks Regional Park, 2145 North Windes Drive, Orange 92869; (714) 973-6620 or (714) 973-6622; www.ocparks.com

Finding the trailhead: From Highway 55 (Newport Freeway), take the Katella Avenue exit and head east on Katella Avenue. Turn left (north) at Windes Drive. The park sign can be easy to miss. Follow Windes Drive to the park gate.

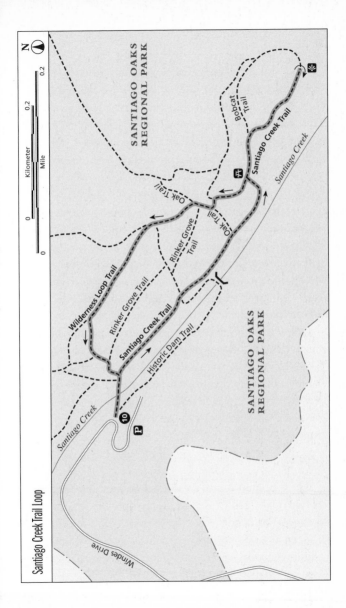

Santiago Creek Trail Loop

The Hike

Santiago Oaks Regional Park rests on a portion of the old Rancho Santiago de Santa Ana, which was granted to Jose Yorba by the Spanish governor Arillaga in 1810. In the late 1800s this area was prowled by several notorious bandits, including Joaquin Murietta and Three-Fingered Jack. The outlaws would sweep down from the hills and terrorize local communities or rob the Butterfield Stage, which passed through the lower Santiago Canyon area.

From the far end of the parking lot, follow the paved trail east past the information sign to a dirt trail, where you turn right. The trail forks at another large sign. Continue straight on the Santiago Creek Trail, which proceeds uphill.

Continue straight past junctions with Sourgrass and Historic Dam Trails when the trail levels. You will soon arrive atop the remnants of a dam originally constructed in 1879.

From here the trail descends slightly, passing a picnic area at 0.5 mile, and eventually reaches a junction with the Oak and Rinker Grove Trails. Continue straight ahead. The trail meanders a bit, eventually reaching a stream crossing (after winter rains, the creek level may preclude a crossing). The trail proceeds through a narrow, water-carved corridor that is covered with lush vines, then heads uphill to where railroad-tie steps lead to a view of Villa Park Dam at 1.0 mile.

Reverse your course to the picnic area and head right onto the Oak Trail, which heads uphill to the right (north). Pass through an open grassy meadow and the wooden fence. At 1.7 miles turn left (west) onto the Wilderness Loop Trail. Follow this trail along rolling terrain past several trail junctions, eventually reaching a concrete bridge and a three-way trail intersection. Head right and take the trail that meanders back west, crossing the creek and climbing up railroad ties to the paved road. Head left along the side of the road to get back to your car.

Miles and Directions

0.0 Start at the paved trail at the end of the parking lot.

0.5 Reach the picnic area.

1.0 The dam comes into view.

1.7 At the junction turn left onto the Wilderness Loop Trail.

2.0 Come to a concrete bridge and three-way intersection. Turn right.

2.2 Arrive back at the parking lot.

11 Peters Canyon Lake Loop

Peters Canyon Regional Park may be small, but it offers great trails, a scenic lake, and a sense of being in the outdoors without straying too far from civilization. This is an easily accessible family hike, with options for longer treks if you wish.

Distance: 2.5-mile loop
Approximate hiking time: 1.25 hours
Difficulty: Easy
Elevation gain: 250 feet
Trail surface: Fire road, some wide footpath
Best season: Fall through spring; early mornings in summer
Other trail users: Mountain bikers, equestrians

Canine compatibility: Dogs not permitted
Fees and permits: $3 parking fee
Schedule: Open 7:00 a.m. to sunset daily
Maps: USGS Orange
Trail contacts: Peters Canyon Regional Park, 8548 Canyon View Avenue, Orange 92869;. (714) 973-6611 or (714) 973-6612; www.ocparks.com

Finding the trailhead: From Highway 55 (Newport Freeway), take the Chapman Avenue exit and head east on Chapman Avenue to Jamboree Boulevard. Turn right (south) onto Jamboree Boulevard; after 0.6 mile turn right onto Canyon View Lane.

From Interstate 5 (Santa Ana Freeway), take Jamboree Boulevard north for 5.3 miles. Turn left onto Canyon View Lane.

The park entrance and parking area are on your left. A fee is required.

The Hike

The sage-covered hills east of Tustin and Orange look out upon the foothills of the Santa Ana Mountains, and despite

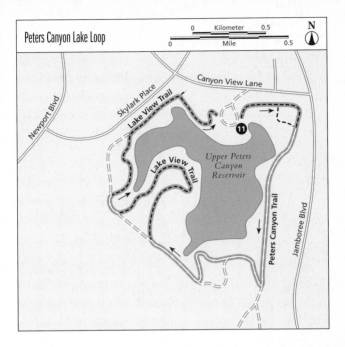

the encroaching development, you can still get a taste of old Orange County. This trail circles the fifty-five-acre Upper Peters Canyon Reservoir, which provides valuable habitat to migrating waterfowl.

The rolling terrain takes you from marsh edge to open hillsides looking east over the lake toward the crest of the northern Santa Anas. This area originally was part of the Spanish Rancho Lomas de Santiago. Later, as part of the Irvine Ranch, it was leased to various farmers. One of these early farmers was James Peters, for whom the canyon is named.

Walk east from the parking lot, turning left on the trail located just before the picnic tables. Turn right on a footpath under the trees or, if it is wet, continue to the corner of Canyon View Lane and Jamboree Boulevard at 0.2 mile and turn right (south).

Reach a fire road and turn right, heading up a short hill to Peters Canyon Trail at 0.5 mile. Turn right again and head down. At the bottom of the hill (0.6 mile), turn right below the dam, then take the right fork up the short, steep hill that sits above the dam. There is a bench at the top of the hill at 1.1 miles.

Turn right and follow the road down and then up again. Turn right onto the Lake View Trail at 1.3 miles, just beyond the crest of the hill. The Lake View Trail heads mostly downhill toward and then along the lakeshore, passing another bench along the way.

At 1.8 miles you will turn right onto a wide path/road. Follow the road as it skirts the lake, then turn right onto a narrowing path. The path runs in and out of brush along the northern shoreline of the reservoir, eventually leading you back to the parking lot.

Miles and Directions

0.0   Start by turning left onto the trail just before the picnic tables.

0.2   Reach the corner of Jamboree Boulevard; turn right (south).

0.5   Arrive at the Peters Canyon Trail junction; turn right and head downhill.

0.6   Turn right (west) below the dam.

1.1   Reach a bench overlooking the reservoir.

1.3   At the Lake View Trail junction, turn right (north).

1.8   Turn right and follow the lakeshore.

2.5   Arrive back at the parking lot.

12 Borrego Canyon to Red Rock Canyon

The trail follows beside, across, and through Borrego Canyon Creek and reaches the more open and undeveloped hillsides. Eventually you strike out onto the narrow and very scenic Red Rock Canyon Trail, which meanders through oak woodland and coastal sage scrub to 100-foot-high red sandstone cliffs in Red Rock Canyon.

Distance: 5.0 miles out and back
Approximate hiking time: 2.5 hours
Difficulty: Moderate
Elevation gain: 460 feet
Trail surface: Wide foot trail up Borrego Canyon, Mustard Trail fire road for a short distance, narrow footpath on Red Rock Canyon Trail
Best season: Fall through spring; early mornings in summer
Other trail users: One-way (uphill) mountain bikers and

equestrians on Borrego Canyon and Mustard Road Trails; hikers only on Red Rock Canyon Trail
Canine compatibility: Dogs not permitted
Fees and permits: $3 parking fee
Schedule: Open 7:00 a.m. to sunset daily
Maps: USGS El Toro
Trail contacts: Limestone Canyon and Whiting Ranch Wilderness Park, P.O. Box 156, Trabuco Canyon 92678; (949) 923-2245; www.ocparks.com/whitingranch

Finding the trailhead: From Interstate 5 (Santa Ana Freeway), take the Bake Parkway exit and go east 4.7 miles to Portola Parkway. Turn left (north) onto Portola Parkway and drive to Marke—the next signal and entrance to the Foothill Ranch Marketplace shopping center. Turn right and then make an immediate left, where you will find

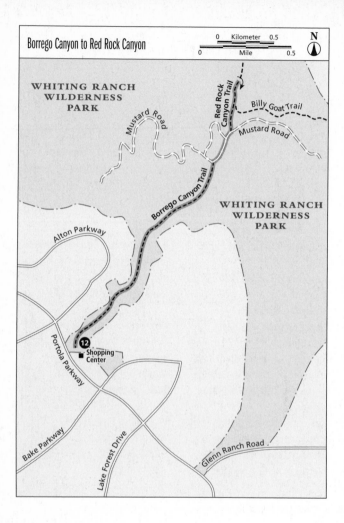

Borrego Canyon to Red Rock Canyon

WHITING RANCH
WILDERNESS
PARK

Mustard Road

Red Rock Canyon Trail

Billy Goat Trail

Mustard Road

Borrego Canyon Trail

WHITING RANCH
WILDERNESS
PARK

Alton Parkway

Portola Parkway

12

Shopping Center

Bake Parkway

Lake Forest Drive

Glenn Ranch Road

0   Kilometer   0.5
0   Mile   0.5

N

parking for Whiting Ranch Wilderness Park. The entrance and trail-head are located at the northern end of the shopping center.

The Hike

Note: In 2007 the Santiago Fire burned nearly 90 percent of the park. As of this writing, the park is open and in the process of natural recovery. Please respect the recovery process by staying on established trails and following park rules.

The trailhead and entrance to Whiting Ranch will not inspire you. It literally is located in a shopping center parking lot. Do not despair. As soon as you descend into Borrego Canyon, the sycamore-shaded trail spirits you far from signs of commerce.

From the trailhead, head downhill about 25 yards until you intersect the Borrego Canyon Trail; bear right (northeast). The wide trail gradually gains elevation. As you continue up the canyon, the trail becomes a narrower footpath and makes several stream crossings. A small footbridge traverses a section of steeper wash. This trail is also a popular mountain bike route (one-way up the canyon). Remember to keep right when hiking this trail to permit safe passing.

The Borrego Canyon Trail stays in the shady canyon bottom under groves of oaks and sycamores. At 1.6 miles the footpath merges with the wide Mustard Road. Turn right (east) onto Mustard Road and walk uphill, passing one trail, until you reach a small wooden footbridge on the left. This is the start of the Red Rock Canyon Trail (1.8 miles).

Cross the bridge and head north through the more open coastal scrub sage and oak woodland along the canyon. You soon reach the upper portions of the canyon, where telltale red sandstone cliffs rise around you. Shaped by water and wind, these cliffs were once the seabed of the shallow ocean that once covered this section of California and were later uplifted by tectonic activity. The trail ends near the top of the canyon at 2.5 miles.

Return to your car the way you came.

Miles and Directions

0.0 Start at the parking area and descend into Borrego Canyon, heading right (east).

1.6 Turn right at the junction with Mustard Road.

1.8 Turn left onto the Red Rock Canyon Trail.

2.5 Reach the end of the trail at the top of the canyon. Retrace your steps to the trailhead.

5.0 Arrive back at the trailhead and parking area.

13 Live Oak Trail

The Live Oak Trail is a combination of wide foot trail and fire road in the western section of O'Neill Regional Park. This hike traverses some of the less traveled and most scenic areas of the park. Despite the trail's proximity to residential development, within minutes from your car you will find yourself in open woodland and grassy meadows. Over the course of 1.5 miles, you climb 600 feet to a spectacular summit and observation point.

Distance: 3.0 miles out and back
Approximate hiking time: 1.3 hours
Difficulty: Moderate
Elevation gain: 600 feet
Trail surface: Dirt trail, fire road
Best season: Fall through spring; early mornings in summer
Other trail users: Mountain bikers, equestrians, trail runners
Canine compatibility: Dogs not permitted
Fees and permits: No fees or permits required
Schedule: Open sunrise to sunset
Maps: USGS Santiago Peak
Trail contacts: O'Neill Regional Park, 30892 Trabuco Canyon Road, Trabuco Canyon 92678; (949) 923-2260 or (949) 923-2256

Finding the trailhead: From Interstates 5 or 405 take Bake Parkway east for 4.7 miles to Portola Parkway. Turn right onto Portola and proceed south for about 1.1 miles to Glenn Ranch Road. Turn left onto Glenn Ranch Road and follow it up and over the hill to where it ends at El Toro Road. Turn left onto El Toro Road and travel for 0.3 mile to the signal at Valley Vista. Make a right-hand (east) turn here and proceed up Valley Vista a short distance to Meadow Ridge. Turn right (south) onto Meadow Ridge and follow the road to its end. Parking is available in a small lot at the end of the street or along

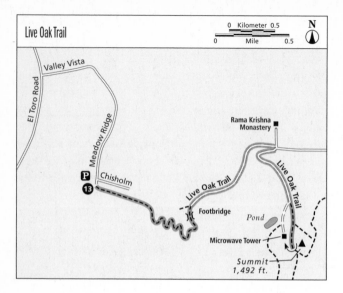

the west side of Meadow Ridge. The trail begins at the very end of Meadow Ridge.

The Hike

From the end of Meadow Ridge, turn left (east) down a paved and dirt service road that provides access to a nursery. A trail sign marks the beginning of the hike. For a few hundred yards, the trail proceeds between the rear of residences and the nursery, but it soon breaks out into the open hills.

A short, steep section of winding trail heads up and over a small hill. Here the coastal woodland is thick with plants and trees. Live oak and toyon (with its characteristic red berries) dominate. Drop down the other side of the ridge through an oak-surrounded meadow and across a small bridge at 0.4 mile. Oak acorns were one of several major food sources for Native Americans living in this region. Ground and then soaked for many days to remove tannins, acorns were used to make flour.

Beyond the bridge turn right (east) onto a fire road. Initially the fire road is steep, but after a short bit it levels and passes through an open valley. Here you will see many artichoke thistle and mustard plants (both invasive, non-native species). A shorter uphill leads to an intersection and fence/road beyond at 1.0 mile. The Rama Krishna Monastery lies on the hill to your left, an easy walk up the paved road beyond the fence.

Before reaching the fence, make a very sharp right-hand turn at the intersection and proceed up the fire road as it curves back left and up. Through the next 0.3 mile, you will see many cacti adjacent to the trail. In fall and winter the purple fruits abound and provide food for wildlife. (Beware: The fruit has many tiny cactus needles and should not be picked.) In late spring, cacti and other native flowers bloom on the hillsides. Off to the left is Saddleback Mountain, with Modjeska Peak on the left and Santiago Peak on the right.

Continue up the fire road to where it levels and another road splits off to your left toward a microwave tower at 1.3 miles. Take the left-hand road, which narrows and heads up a last steep incline to the high point (1,492 feet) at the top of the hill at 1.5 miles. There are several picnic tables, directed views to Catalina and other spots, and a nice plaque describing the 360-degree view that runs from Saddleback in the northeast to the San Joaquin Hills in the west. Retrace the route back to your car.

Miles and Directions

0.0 Start at the end of Meadow Ridge and turn left (east) down a service road.

0.4 Cross the footbridge and turn right (east), heading uphill.

1.0 Make a sharp right turn (uphill/south).

1.3 Take the left fork to the summit.

1.5 Enjoy the view from the top before retracing your steps.

3.0 Arrive back at the trailhead and your car.

14 Riley Wilderness Park Loop

This hike circumnavigates most of Thomas F. Riley Wilderness Park and takes you on a tour of the best trails. You will climb up and down through this rolling landscape, amid ancient oaks in the low valleys and atop grassy hilltops.

Distance: 2.7-mile loop

Approximate hiking time: 1.5 hours

Difficulty: Easy

Elevation gain: 450 feet

Trail surface: Fire road, some footpath

Best season: Fall through spring; early mornings in summer

Other trail users: Mountain bikers, equestrians, trail runners

Canine compatibility: Dogs not permitted

Fees and permits: $3 parking (dollar bills only)

Schedule: Open 7:00 a.m. to sunset daily

Maps: USGS Cañada Gobernadora

Trail contacts: Thomas F. Riley Wilderness Park, 30952 Oso Parkway, Coto de Caza 92679; (949) 923-2265 or (949) 923-2266; www.ocparks.com

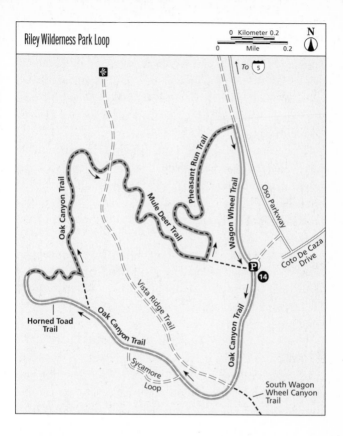

0 Kilometer 0.2

0 Mile 0.2

N

Oak Canyon Trail

Mule Deer Trail

Pheasant Run Trail

Wagon Wheel Trail

Oso Parkway

↑ *To* 5

Coto De Caza Drive

P 14

Vista Ridge Trail

Horned Toad Trail

Oak Canyon Trail

Oak Canyon Trail

Sycamore Loop

South Wagon Wheel Canyon Trail

Finding the trailhead: From Interstate 5 (Santa Ana Freeway), take the Oso Parkway exit and drive east on Oso Parkway for 6 miles. The park entrance (a right-hand turn) lies 50 yards before the stop sign at Oso Parkway and Coto De Caza Drive. A short dirt road (0.2 mile) leads to the parking area and ranger station. There is a $3 per vehicle fee. A toilet and bulletin board are the only facilities available. No water or camping facilities are available in the park.

The Hike

Thomas F. Riley Wilderness Park is a spare 475 acres of rolling sage-covered hills and oak and sycamore–shaded valleys. It was officially opened in 1994 as Wagon Wheel Wilderness Park and later renamed for a former Orange County supervisor.

The park contains a host of pleasant and usually uncrowded trails. Many people hope that more of the beautiful surrounding hills and valleys will be preserved and added to this small park. Barring this, Riley Park may become only a curious anomaly in an otherwise barren landscape of ubiquitous development.

From the parking area, head south past the bulletin board on the Oak Canyon Trail. Soon the Vista Ridge Trail heads right (northwest) and South Wagon Wheel Canyon Trail heads left. Continue straight ahead, passing the Sycamore Loop turnoff on your left (south) at 0.3 mile.

The Oak Canyon Trail takes a right-hand turn under the oaks; head straight (west) on the Horned Toad Trail at 0.7 mile, walking up the hill. At the top of the hill, you will enjoy good views of most of the park. Continue on the Horned Toad Trail as it turns right (east) and winds back down to Oak Canyon Trail at 1.0 mile.

Turn left (north), following Oak Canyon Trail past a pond. Cross a creek and ascend to the Vista Ridge Trail fire road at 1.5 miles. Directly across the fire road is the top of Mule Deer Trail, a narrow footpath. Follow this down into a small valley to a junction with the Pheasant Run Trail, which heads uphill on your left (north) at 1.9 miles. Follow the Pheasant Run Trail over a low hill, then back down to where it ends at the Wagon Wheel Trail.

Turn right (south) onto the Wagon Wheel Trail at 2.3 miles as it heads under the shade of old oak trees back to the trailhead.

Miles and Directions

0.0 Start at the parking area and head south past the bulletin board on the Oak Canyon Trail.

0.3 Stay right at the Sycamore Loop turnoff.

0.7 At the junction, head straight on the Horned Toad Trail.

1.0 Rejoin the Oak Canyon Trail and turn left (north).

1.5 Reach an intersection with the Vista Ridge and Mule Deer Trails; follow the Mule Deer Trail.

1.9 Turn left (north) onto Pheasant Run Trail.

2.3 Turn right (south) onto Wagon Wheel Trail.

2.7 Arrive back at the parking area.

15 West Ridge and Oak Trail Loop

Though not a long hike, the varied terrain, excellent vistas, and general lack of traffic make this one of the premier hikes in Ronald W. Caspers Wilderness Park. Summer in Caspers Park, particularly on the exposed ridges traversed on this hike, can be unpleasant and enervating. Fall, winter, and spring are ideal for hiking here.

Distance: 3.4-mile loop
Approximate hiking time: 1.75 hours
Difficulty: Moderate
Elevation gain: 360 feet
Trail surface: Fire road, footpath
Best season: Fall through spring; early mornings in summer
Other trail users: Mountain bikers, equestrians
Canine compatibility: Dogs not permitted

Fees and permits: $5 parking fee
Schedule: Open 7:00 a.m. to sunset daily; camping available
Maps: USGS Cañada Gobernadora
Trail contacts: Ronald W. Caspers Wilderness Park, 33401 Ortega Highway (mailing address: P.O. Box 395), San Juan Capistrano 92675; (949) 923-2210; www.ocparks.com

Finding the trailhead: From Interstate 5 (Santa Ana Freeway), take the Ortega Highway (Highway 74) east for 7.6 miles. The park entrance is on your left (north). To reach the Dick Loskorn trailhead, drive north past the park entrance and visitor center to the end of the paved road; turn left at the windmills. The trail is marked NATURE TRAIL and begins on the west side of the parking area.

The Hike

Ronald W. Caspers Wilderness Park consists of 8,000 acres that straddle Ortega Highway in the western foothills of the

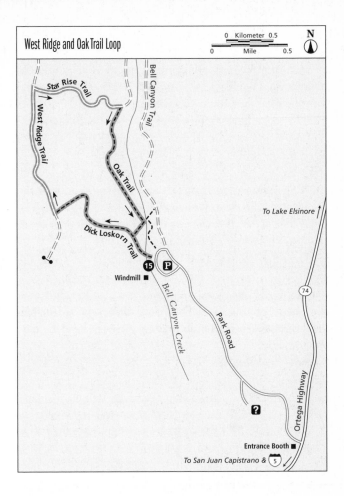

Santa Ana Mountains. Public access is permitted only in the northern part of the park. Here you will find many valleys and hills featuring coastal live oak, California sycamore, and coastal scrub sage. In the winter and spring, running streams and seasonal wildflowers add to the enjoyment of a visit. Mountain lions are commonly present, and care should be taken to not let small children stray from your group. On Saturday and Sunday (9:00 a.m. to 3:00 p.m.), you can also visit the park's interpretive center.

The beginning and end of this hike pass under tall sycamores and ancient oak trees. The initial climb up to the West Ridge on the Dick Loskorn Trail winds up a ridge of soft, exposed sandstone cliffs. Care should be taken here. Once the wide West Ridge Trail is reached, you hike the high ridge north, with unsurpassed views east and west. The descent back into Bell Canyon takes you on a quiet footpath that leads back to your starting point.

From the Nature Trail sign, head northwest across the Bell Canyon creekbed into the oak woods, passing a park bench. At 0.1 mile you will turn left at the junction with the Dick Loskorn Trail. Head west under the trees, then break out onto a sandstone ridge, which can be quite narrow in places.

After a continuous climb you reach the West Ridge Trail fire road at 0.8 mile. Follow the West Ridge Trail right (north). Enjoy good views east into Bell Canyon and west into the still-undeveloped Cañada Gobernadora.

After traveling about 0.8 mile north on the West Ridge Trail, turn right (east) at the junction onto Star Rise Trail at 1.6 miles. Star Rise Trail, a fire road, descends at a gradual incline east into Bell Canyon. After reaching the canyon bottom at 2.3 miles, turn right (south) onto the Oak Trail.

The Oak Trail is a lightly traveled footpath under oaks and sycamores that roughly parallels the Bell Canyon creekbed and returns you to the Dick Loskorn Trail junction. From here retrace your route back to your car.

Miles and Directions

0.0 Start at the NATURE TRAIL sign.

0.1 Head left (northwest) on the Dick Loskorn Trail.

0.8 Reach the West Ridge Trail and turn right (north).

1.6 Descend on the Star Rise Trail.

2.3 Reach the Oak Trail junction and go right (south).

3.3 Turn right onto the Dick Loskorn Trail.

3.4 Arrive back at the trailhead.

The Mountains

The Santa Ana Mountains are a dominant backdrop for Orange County—scenically, geographically, and historically. The two highest peaks, Santiago and Modjeska, form the distinctive "Old Saddleback," whose silhouette can be seen from throughout the county. These high peaks, and most of the Santa Ana high country, lie within the confines of the Cleveland National Forest. A wide variety of footpaths, fire roads, and paved roads crisscross the range, and abundant hiking opportunities exist here. Wildlife is also varied. The Santa Anas are seasonal or permanent home to hundreds of bird species; dozens of mammal, reptile, and amphibian species; and seven species of fish. Mountain lions are found in many areas.

The Santa Ana Mountains can be quite rugged, with high ridges and deep canyons. Due to the density of coastal chaparral, travel off established trails can be extremely difficult. At 5,687 feet, the highest point, Santiago Peak, is not particularly lofty. However, the weather high above the coastal plains can be both extremely warm and extremely cold. These mountains are not to be taken lightly.

Parking in day-use areas of Cleveland National Forest requires the purchase and display of a Forest Adventure Pass. Day-use and annual passes can be purchased at USDA Forest Service offices and most outdoor stores.

16 Silverado Canyon–Silverado Motorway

This hike on the "motorway" (a footpath) takes you from upper Silverado Canyon to a ridgetop view of the Pacific Ocean. Though the incline is never great, it is a steady climb up the canyon wall. The views into Silverado Canyon toward Old Saddleback and westward become grander the higher you climb.

Distance: 4.4 miles out and back
Approximate hiking time: 2.2 hours
Difficulty: Moderate
Elevation gain: 520 feet
Trail surface: Fire road, eroded fire road/footpath
Best season: Fall through spring; early mornings in summer
Other trail users: Mountain bikers, equestrians
Canine compatibility: Dogs permitted
Fees and permits: Forest Adventure Pass required—$5 for day pass, $30 per year
Schedule: No set schedule
Maps: USGS Santiago Peak, Corona South
Trail contacts: Cleveland National Forest, Trabuco Ranger District, 1147 East Sixth Street, Corona 92879; (951) 736-1811; www.fs .fed.us/r5/cleveland

Finding the trailhead: From Highway 55 (Newport Freeway), take Chapman Avenue east to Jamboree Boulevard. Proceed straight; Chapman becomes Santiago Canyon Road. Drive 6.7 miles southeast on Santiago Canyon Road and turn left onto Silverado Canyon Road. Follow Silverado Canyon Road east for 5.4 miles to a parking area and USDA Forest Service gate.

From Interstate 5 (Santa Ana Freeway), go east 13.6 miles on El Toro Road/Santiago Canyon Road. At Silverado Canyon Road turn right (east) and travel for 5.4 miles to the parking area.

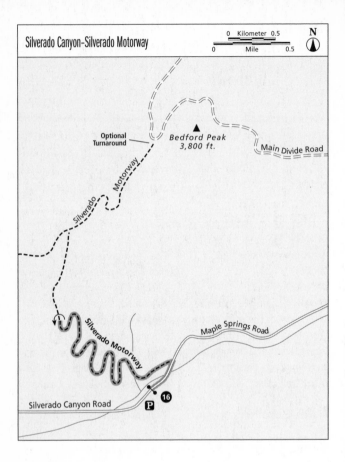

0   Kilometer   0.5

0   Mile   0.5

N

Optional
Turnaround

Bedford Peak
3,800 ft.

Main Divide Road

Silverado Motorway

Silverado Motorway

Maple Springs Road

Silverado Canyon Road

P   16

The Hike

Today the Silverado Motorway is a footpath that makes
broad switchbacks up the sage and chaparral–covered canyon wall toward Bedford Peak. Once a fire road, the trail

has so deteriorated over the years that it is difficult to believe it was once passable by vehicles. The motorway switchbacks up the side of Silverado Canyon, eventually reaching the crest of a high ridge separating Ladd and Silverado Canyons. A mile farther up the ridge trail lies the Main Divide Road; a short distance farther is the summit of Bedford Peak, one of the higher summits in the Santa Ana Mountains. This hike is quite exposed and should be avoided in hot weather.

Begin at the USDA Forest Service gate and proceed up the Maple Springs (Silverado Canyon) Road until you reach a stream at 0.1 mile. Cross the stream and proceed up the canyon for approximately 100 yards. The Silverado Motorway footpath is on your left; go westward up this trail.

The trail cuts north up a side canyon. In winter, both this side canyon and the trail run with water. Cross the waterway, if in season, and begin your journey upward. The trail is eroded in places.

After several switchbacks you reach a rocky flat where the trail cuts back east up toward the ridge. Continue up the trail as it proceeds east up the side of the ridge.

At 2.2 miles you reach a large flat area on the ridgetop. Explore the views from various aspects of the ridge before heading back the way you came to the shady bottom of Silverado Canyon.

Option

If you feel energized, continue on the trail as it heads east along the ridge. At the 3.3-mile mark, intersect Main Divide Road. Either return along the path you've already followed or continue an extra 0.5 mile up and right (east) on Main Divide Road to Bedford Peak (3,800 feet).

Miles and Directions

0.0 Start at the USDA Forest Service gate and proceed up the road.

0.1 Cross a creek.

0.1+ Take the footpath on the left.

2.2 Reach a large flat area with excellent views to the west. Retrace your steps.

4.4 Arrive back at the parking area and your vehicle.

17 Santiago Trail

Although the Santiago Trail leads 8.0 miles to Old Camp in the upper reaches of Modjeska (Santiago) Canyon, this hike only proceeds up the first 2.5 miles. From the high turnaround point you will enjoy sweeping views out toward the San Joaquin Hills near Laguna Beach and into the wild upper reaches of Modjeska Canyon.

Distance: 5.0 miles out and back

Approximate hiking time: 2.5 hours

Difficulty: Moderate

Elevation gain: 600 feet

Trail surface: Fire road, wide trail

Best season: Fall through spring; early mornings in summer

Other trail users: Mountain bikers, equestrians, trail runners

Canine compatibility: Dogs permitted

Fees and permits: No fees or permits required

Schedule: No set hours

Maps: USGS El Toro, Santiago Peak

Trail contacts: Cleveland National Forest, Trabuco Ranger District, 1147 East Sixth Street, Corona 92879; (951) 736-1811; www.fs .fed.us/r5/cleveland

Finding the trailhead: From Interstate 5 (Santa Ana Freeway), take El Toro Road (which becomes Santiago Canyon Road) eastward for approximately 8.9 miles; turn right at the Modjeska Grade Road turnoff. This right-hand turn is located about 1.3 miles past the Live Oak Canyon Road turnoff (also known as Cook's Corner). Park well off the road surface near the bottom of Modjeska Grade Road toward its junction with Santiago Canyon Road. No parking is permitted higher up the road.

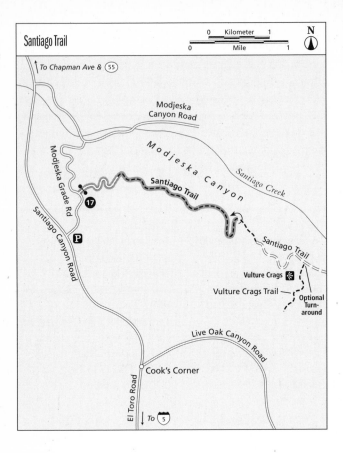

Santiago Trail

| 0 | Kilometer | 1 |

| 0 | Mile | 1 |

N

↑ To Chapman Ave & 55

Modjeska Canyon Road

Modjeska Canyon

Santiago Creek

Modjeska Grade Rd

17

Santiago Trail

P

Santiago Canyon Road

Santiago Trail

Vulture Crags

Vulture Crags Trail

Optional Turn-around

Live Oak Canyon Road

Cook's Corner

El Toro Road

↓ To 5

The Hike

The Santiago Trail is a former fire road that has been encouraged to revert to a nice foot trail. Occasionally the trail is graded, and conditions may vary. The entire area traversed by this hike was burned by the 2007 Santiago Fire.

You can observe the regenerative forces of nature at work as plants and animals reestablish themselves.

From your car proceed up Modjeska Grade Road to a point just below its crest. A steel gate and the trailhead are on your right. Respect any fire or other closure signs; if none are posted, go east up the fire road as it runs along the side of the ridge. At a sharp left turn, you gain a good view to the southwest.

A short distance farther, the trail narrows and you get your first glimpse to the northeast into Modjeska Canyon. Stay on the main trail where various informal trails head up the steep ridge.

The main trail passes along the north side of the ridgeline, affording unobstructed views into Modjeska Canyon and toward the twin peaks of Old Saddleback. The trail gently descends a bit, then begins to climb a grade on the west side of the ridge. At the top of the incline, the trail levels, drops some, and then rounds another bend. Stay left on the main trail where a footpath descends right.

Continue along the Santiago Trail. At 2.5 miles, about 150 yards past a sharp switchback, you will reach a level spot. At this spot, the end point of this hike, you may enjoy good views into the upper reaches of Modjeska Canyon. Return the way you came.

Option

The Vulture Crags are less than 1.0 mile beyond the turnaround point of this hike. These conglomerate cliffs were once a roosting place for the endangered California condor. Like the grizzly bear, also once a resident of the Santa Ana Mountains, the condor was laid low by rifle bullets and poison. Deep in the recesses of the upper Modjeska Canyon, evidence of mining activity from the 1870s can still be found, including old mining trails and mineshafts.

To visit Vulture Crags, proceed from the level turnaround spot up the Santiago Trail to a point where a long descent begins. After 0.6 mile the trail rapidly descends to a level area along the ridge. Here you can look west and see Vulture Crags. Return via the same route.

Miles and Directions

0.0   Start at the steel gate and go east up the fire road.

0.6   Stay on the main trail, ignoring the many informal trails.

1.6   Stay left on the main trail where a footpath descends right.

2.5   Reach a level spot and enjoy the views into Modjeska Canyon. This is your turnaround point.

5.0   Arrive back at the trailhead.

18 Holy Jim Trail

The hike into Holy Jim Canyon is one of the most scenic and interesting in the Santa Ana Mountains. The hike passes under a multitude of trees and crosses Holy Jim Creek many times before eventually reaching the falls, a 35-foot cascade and popular picnic spot.

Distance: 2.7 miles out and back
Approximate hiking time: 1.5 hours
Difficulty: Easy
Elevation gain: 620 feet
Trail surface: Footpath
Best season: Fall through spring; early mornings in summer
Other trail users: Mountain bikers
Canine compatibility: Dogs permitted
Fees and permits: Forest Adventure Pass required—$5 for day pass; $30 per year
Schedule: No set hours
Maps: USGS Santiago Peak
Trail contacts: Cleveland National Forest, Trabuco Ranger District, 1147 East Sixth Street, Corona 92879; (951) 736-1811; www.fs.fed.us/r5/cleveland

Finding the trailhead: From Interstate 5 (Santa Ana Freeway), take El Toro Road east for 7.6 miles. Turn right (east) onto Live Oak Canyon Road and travel south and east for 4.4 miles. Make a left-hand (east) turn onto Trabuco Creek Road (6S13) and follow this bumpy dirt road east for 4.7 miles to the Holy Jim Canyon Road (6S14) turnoff. Park in the large flat area at the intersection of Trabuco Creek and Holy Jim Canyon Roads. *Do not* drive up Holy Jim Canyon Road—traffic is restricted to local residents.

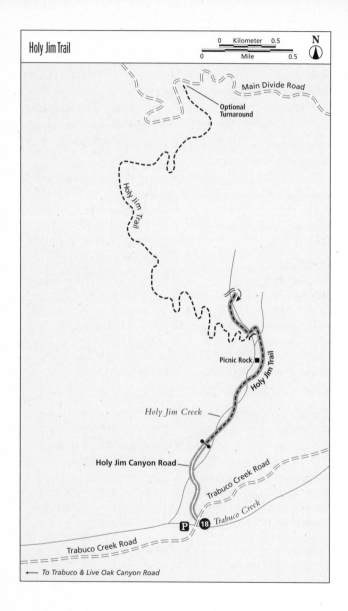

Holy Jim Trail

0   Kilometer   0.5

0   Mile   0.5

N

Main Divide Road

Optional
Turnaround

Holy Jim Trail

Picnic Rock

Holy Jim Trail

Holy Jim Creek

Holy Jim Canyon Road

Trabuco Creek Road

Trabuco Creek

P   18   Trabuco Creek

Trabuco Creek Road

← To Trabuco & Live Oak Canyon Road

The Hike

Holy Jim Canyon is named for James T. Smith, a canyon resident and beekeeper during the late 1800s who was renowned for his foul language. Smith was variously nicknamed "Cussin' Jim," "Lyin' Jim," "Greasy Jim," and "Salvation Jim," but government mapmakers bestowed the sanitized "Holy Jim" on the canyon with which he was closely associated. The numerous fig trees found throughout the canyon are the wild descendants of Smith's fig orchard, which, along with his house, burned in a 1908 fire.

From the parking area begin walking left (north) up Holy Jim Canyon Road (6S14) to the Holy Jim trailhead at 0.5 mile. The trail meanders up the canyon, alternating between shade and sun. After the second stream crossing, you may see a stone wall, the only remnants of Jim Smith's cabin. Poison oak is common on this route, so stay on the trail and be sure you know how to identify this plant.

Further along the trail you can glimpse Santiago Peak far up the ridge to your left (north). Continue up the trail until you reach a clearing. Picnic Rock is on your left (west) at 1.1 mile, and the large oak to the right (east) is thought to be over 500 years old.

The trail soon makes a final stream crossing (to the west side of the canyon); a small stone "check dam" is found here. Once you cross to the opposite side of the creek, the trail splits. Take the right fork and continue upstream; swarms of ladybugs can be found along the trail in spring and summer. After 400 yards the trail ends at the falls at 1.4 miles.

Head back the way you came, enjoying the scenery and gentle downhill grade as you return to your starting point.

Option

A more challenging 10.0-mile hike leads up toward the higher reaches of Old Saddleback. From the trail intersection 400 yards below the falls, take the left-hand fork. The trail quickly switchbacks up the steep western slope of Holy Jim Canyon. Eventually the trail contours along the canyon wall and terminates at the Main Divide Road, some 2,000 vertical feet higher. Summer sun should be avoided; spring brings a number of bright wildflowers.

Miles and Directions

0.0 Start at the parking area and begin walking left (north) up Holy Jim Canyon Road.

0.5 Reach the Holy Jim trailhead.

0.7 Pass some fig trees, remnants of an old orchard.

1.1 Pass Picnic Rock on your left.

1.4 Reach the waterfall and your turnaround point.

2.8 Arrive back at the parking area.

19 Trabuco Trail

Unlike Holy Jim Canyon, there is no waterfall on the Trabuco Trail to attract the crowds. But the area is more open and affords better views into the surrounding mountain terrain. The spring wildflower displays along Trabuco Creek are some of the finest in the entire Santa Ana range. Most of the trail is exposed to direct sun, so pick a cooler day for this hike.

Distance: 3.6 miles out and back
Approximate hiking time: 1.8 hours
Difficulty: Moderate
Elevation gain: 880 feet
Trail surface: Smooth to rugged footpath, stream crossings
Best season: Fall through spring; early mornings in summer
Other trail users: Mountain bikers, equestrians, trail runners

Canine compatibility: Dogs permitted
Fees and permits: Forest Adventure Pass required—$5 for day pass; $30 per year
Schedule: No set hours
Maps: USGS Alberhill
Trail contacts: Cleveland National Forest, Trabuco Ranger District, 1147 East Sixth Street Corona 92879; (951) 736-1811; www.fs.fed.us/r5/cleveland

Finding the trailhead: From Interstate 5 (Santa Ana Freeway), take El Toro Road east for 7.6 miles. Turn right (east) onto Live Oak Canyon Road and travel south and east for 4.4 miles. Make a left-hand (east) turn onto Trabuco Creek Road (6S13) and follow this bumpy dirt road for 5.7 miles (past the Holy Jim Canyon turnoff) to its end at a USDA Forest Service gate. The trail starts here. Parking is limited. If no parking is available at the trailhead, park back at the large flat area at the intersection of Trabuco Creek and Holy Jim Canyon Roads.

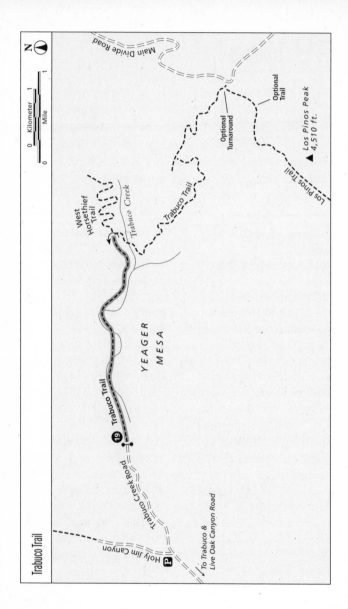

Trabuco Trail

Main Divide Road

West Horsethief Trail

Trabuco Creek

Trabuco Trail

Optional Turnaround

Optional Trail

Los Pinos Trail

Los Pinos Peak
4,510 ft.

N

0   Kilometer   1

0   Mile   1

YEAGER MESA

Trabuco Trail

19

Trabuco Creek Road

Holy Jim Canyon

P

To Trabuco &
Live Oak Canyon Road

The Hike

Although the drive up the dirt Trabuco Creek Road to the trailhead can be bumpy—and is not advisable during a heavy runoff—the hiking in Holy Jim Canyon and the less-traveled Trabuco Canyon exhibits a remoteness and primitive character seldom found on such a short hike.

The trail begins out of a small parking area at the very end of Trabuco Creek Road. A metal post and logs may mark this spot. After leaving the parking area, the nice footpath heads under large oak trees and then into more open terrain alongside Trabuco Creek. The trail crosses the creekbed a few times, then closely follows the left (north) side of the creek. In spring the next mile or so of trail is bounded by many varieties of wildflowers.

As you hike on the left side of the trail, you pass near an old mine entrance in the adjacent hillside. Yeager Mesa, a private inholding and pristine oak-surrounded meadow, is on the right (south) side of the creek at 0.9 mile. Eventually the trail passes into the shade of trees along the creek. Under a tree canopy at 1.8 miles, a sign marks the split of the Trabuco Trail, which crosses the stream to the right (south), and the West Horsethief Trail, which climbs up switchbacks on the left (north). This is a nice place to picnic and enjoy the shaded quiet.

After relaxing, return to your car the way you came.

Options

You can lengthen this hike by choosing either of two options. From the juncture of the Trabuco and West Horsethief Trails, cross the stream to your right (south) and pick up the Trabuco Trail again. The Trabuco Trail gradually rises up the canyon above the creek. At the 3.3-mile mark, the trail appears to split on the ridge; stay right. Soon the path becomes very shaded, and at 4.4 miles you arrive at the Main Divide Road.

Either return the way you came (an 8.8-mile out-and-back hike), or continue from this trail intersection by following a footpath, the Los Pinos Trail, that heads right (south) from the junction. Follow the trail along the ridge for 1.1 miles to the 4,510-foot summit of Los Pinos Peak (Hike 22) and enjoy the spectacular view. Return the way you came for an 11.0-mile out-and-back trek.

Miles and Directions

0.0   Start at the small parking area at the end of Trabuco Creek Road.

0.9   Pass Yeager Mesa on the right (south) side of the canyon.

1.8   Reach the west Horsethief Trail junction. Relax awhile before retracing your steps.

3.6   Arrive back at the parking area.

20 San Juan Loop Trail

This trail takes you to a variety of coastal mountain habitats, including seasonal waterfalls, dense mature-oak woodlands, and open chaparral-covered hillsides. Although best tackled in the cooler months, an early-morning start in summer is bound to be pleasant and will allow you to see birds and animals when they are most active.

Distance: 2.2-mile loop

Approximate hiking time: 1.2 hours

Difficulty: Easy

Elevation gain: 320 feet

Trail surface: Smooth to rugged footpath

Best season: Fall through spring; early mornings in summer

Other trail users: Mountain bikers on parts of the trail, trail runners

Canine compatibility: Dogs permitted

Fees and permits: Forest Adventure Pass required—$5 for day pass; $30 per year

Schedule: No set hours

Maps: USGS Sitton Peak

Trail contacts: Cleveland National Forest, Trabuco Ranger District, 1147 East Sixth Street, Corona 92879; (951) 736-1811; www.fs.fed.us/r5/cleveland

Finding the trailhead: From Interstate 5 (Santa Ana Freeway) in San Juan Capistrano, drive approximately 19.5 miles east on the Ortega Highway (Highway 74). The Ortega Oaks Country Store will be on your right (east). Park across the highway in a USDA Forest Service parking area. The trail begins on the right (north) side of the parking area, near the access to the highway.

The Hike

Six mountain streams merge along this short hike to form San Juan Creek, a major county waterway. San Juan Creek

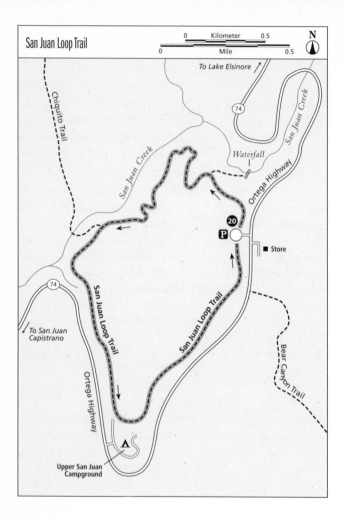

San Juan Loop Trail

Kilometer
0   0.5
Mile
0   0.5

N

To Lake Elsinore

74

San Juan Creek

Chiquito Trail

San Juan Creek

Waterfall

Ortega Highway

20

P

Store

74

To San Juan
Capistrano

San Juan Loop Trail

San Juan Loop Trail

Bear Canyon Trail

Ortega Highway

Upper San Juan
Campground

flows west to join Trabuco Creek at Mission San Juan Capistrano. The granite rocks that line the narrow canyons and dot the hillsides extend southeast through the San Mateo Wilderness. San Juan Canyon was a traditional Native American travel route through the dense chaparral and over the Santa Ana Mountains.

Start your hike on the right (north) side of the parking area. The trail begins with a slight climb, but soon you begin to descend into a rocky canyon. A spur trail on your right makes a short but worthwhile side trip to a seasonal waterfall and rock pools at 0.2 mile. Visit the falls, then continue down the main trail along a series of switchbacks until the trail straightens and levels.

Proceed under a canopy of old oaks along the side of the stream until you reach the junction with the Chiquito Trail at 1.2 miles. Stay to the left and continue on the pleasant, shady trail to Upper San Juan Campground. Again stay left, passing behind the campground at 1.5 miles, and follow a wide section of trail that climbs back into more open terrain. A gentle but constant climb brings you back to the west end of the parking area at 2.2 miles.

Miles and Directions

0.0 Start at right (north) end of the parking area.
0.2 Pass a small seasonal waterfall and rock pools.
1.2 Reach the junction with the Chiquito Trail and stay left (southwest).
1.5 Pass behind the Upper San Juan Campground.
2.2 Arrive back at the parking area.

21 Bear Canyon Trail

This trail takes you from the busy Ortega Highway corridor into the San Mateo Canyon Wilderness. Incredible vistas of some of the wildest sections of the Santa Ana Mountains are your reward. Despite the relatively short nature of the hike, you very quickly lose all signs of civilization.

Distance: 4.0 miles out and back

Approximate hiking time: 2 hours

Difficulty: Moderate

Elevation gain: 720 feet

Trail surface: Smooth to rugged footpath

Best season: Fall through spring; early mornings in summer

Other trail users: Mountain bikers on parts of the trail, trail runners

Canine compatibility: Dogs not permitted

Fees and permits: Forest Adventure Pass required—$5 for day pass; $30 per year

Schedule: No set hours

Maps: USGS Sitton Peak

Trail contacts: Cleveland National Forest, Trabuco Ranger District, 1147 East Sixth Street, Corona 92879; (951) 736-1811; www.fs.fed.us/r5/cleveland

Finding the trailhead: From Interstate 5 (Santa Ana Freeway) in San Juan Capistrano, drive approximately 19.5 miles east on the Ortega Highway (Highway 74). The Ortega Oaks Country Store will be on your right (east). Park across the highway in a USDA Forest Service parking area; this is also the parking area for the San Juan Loop Trail (Hike 20). The trail begins on the east side of the highway, about 75 yards southwest of the store.

The Hike

Like many Santa Ana Mountains hikes, the Bear Canyon Trail is best in the cooler spring, fall, or winter months.

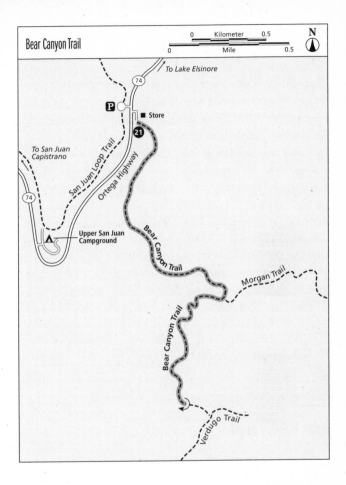

Only portions of the trail pass under ancient stands of oak trees; most of the hike proceeds along exposed chaparral-covered hillsides.

The Bear Canyon Trail is also a great way to familiar-ize yourself with some of the natural history of the Santa

Ana Mountains. Picnic tables outside the Ortega Oaks Country Store make a great place to relax at the end of your journey.

From the trailhead walk a short distance to a backcountry registration station and sign in. From here the trail climbs up and right (east) along the open hillside, eventually crossing under a granite pinnacle.

Continue up along the hillside through decomposing granite until the trail levels. The highway is now lost to view and out of earshot; the going is largely flat, with views to open chaparral-laden hillsides. Cross a seasonal stream at 0.8 mile, then pass a wilderness boundary sign and into the shade of oak and sycamore trees.

Continue under the trees along the valley bottom until you reach the junction with the Morgan Trail at 1.0 mile. Head right, staying on the Bear Canyon Trail as it begins to climb up the hillside. At the crest of the hill at 2.0 miles, enjoy the views to the south and west into the depths of the San Mateo Canyon Wilderness.

Return along the same route, making sure to turn left at the Morgan Trail junction. The mostly downhill trek back to the trailhead goes quickly.

Miles and Directions

0.0   Start at the trailhead on the east side of the highway.

0.8   Cross a seasonal stream.

1.0   Arrive at the Morgan Trail junction. Head right to stay on the Bear Canyon Trail.

2.0   Reach the crest of the hill. Enjoy the views before retracing your steps.

4.0   Arrive back at the trailhead.

22 Los Pinos Peak

This trail takes you to the top of Los Pinos Peak, a wild and high point in the Santa Ana Mountains. Fantastic 360-degree views ranging from the Pacific Ocean to the San Bernardino, San Gabriel, and San Jacinto Mountains await on clear winter days.

Distance: 4.4 miles out and back
Approximate hiking time: 2 hours
Difficulty: Moderate
Elevation gain: 920 feet
Trail surface: Fire road, smooth to rugged footpath
Best season: Fall through spring; early mornings in summer
Other trail users: Mountain bikers, trail runners

Canine compatibility: Dogs permitted
Fees and permits: Forest Adventure Pass required—$5 for day pass; $30 per year
Schedule: No set hours
Maps: USGS Alberhill
Trail contacts: Cleveland National Forest, Trabuco Ranger District, 1147 East Sixth Street, Corona 92879; (951) 736-1811; www.fs.fed.us/r5/cleveland

Finding the trailhead: From Interstate 5 (Santa Ana Freeway), take the Ortega Highway (Highway 74) east for 21.9 miles to Long Canyon Road. Turn left (north) and follow this paved road for 3.5 miles (passing the entrance to Blue Jay Campground) until you reach Main Divide Road. Make a sharp left (west) and drive 0.5 mile up Main Divide Road to a metal gate. Park off to the right (east), taking care not to block the gate or the road. If the gate is open, you can shorten the hike by 1.1 miles by driving to the Los Pinos Saddle.

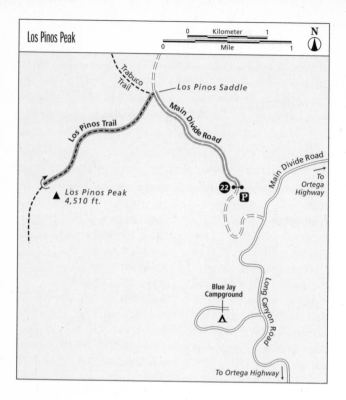

0 Kilometer 1
0 Mile 1

N

Trabuco Trail

Los Pinos Saddle

Los Pinos Trail

Main Divide Road

Main Divide Road

To Ortega Highway

Los Pinos Peak
4,510 ft.

22 P

Blue Jay
Campground

Long Canyon Road

To Ortega Highway

The Hike

At 4,510 feet, Los Pinos Peak is the fourth-highest summit
in the Santa Ana Mountains, yet it is one of the wildest and
least visited of the range's high points. Despite its elevation,
Los Pinos lies within easy reach of the more determined
hiker, who will be rewarded with one of the best vistas
in Southern California. On clear days you can look west-

ward across miles of mountains, foothills, and valleys to the Pacific Ocean. To the east lies Lake Elsinore, with the high peaks of the San Jacinto and San Gabriel Mountains rising in the distance. In spring, wildflowers, green hillsides, and the snowcapped peaks of distant mountains are common sights. Summer can be brutally hot, and winter storms may bring a light covering of snow to Los Pinos.

From the gate, begin hiking up the dirt Main Divide fire road. As you ascend along the west and east sides of the mountain ridge, you begin to gain good views as well as elevation. Continue up the fire road until you reach Los Pinos Saddle, a large flat area with several metal guardrails.

The Los Pinos and Trabuco Trails join Main Divide Road on your left (west) at 1.1 miles. Start the Los Pinos Trail where the Trabuco Trail hits Main Divide Road, but head up the path on the left (south). The Los Pinos Trail winds around the north and west sides of the hillside, eventually joining the exposed ridge.

Continue to gain elevation up the wide ridge trail to a high point (4,489 feet). From here the ridge trail dips slightly, then gains a bit to eventually reach the top of Los Pinos Peak (4,510 feet) at 2.2 miles. Soak up the view and look for the USGS benchmarks on the rocky summit just south of the trail. Turn around and return the way you came, gliding downhill to your car.

Miles and Directions

0.0 Start at the gate on Main Divide Road. (**Option:** If the gate is open, continue driving on Main Divide Road to the junction with the Los Pinos Trail and start hiking at Milepoint 1.1.)

1.1 Reach the junction of the Los Pinos Trail and Main Divide Road; head left (south) and up on the Los Pinos Trail.

2.2 Reach the summit of Los Pinos Peak, your turnaround point.

4.4 Arrive back at the gate and trailhead.

23 El Cariso Nature Trail

El Cariso Nature Trail is an ideal short hike for families. With striking vistas to the north, west, and south, it winds around a large knoll above the El Cariso Ranger Station, which is just south of the Ortega Highway.

Distance: 1.4-mile loop
Approximate hiking time: 45 minutes
Difficulty: Easy
Elevation gain: 120 feet
Trail surface: Smooth footpath
Best season: Fall through spring; early mornings in summer
Other trail users: None
Canine compatibility: Dogs not permitted
Fees and permits: No fees or permits required
Schedule: No set hours
Maps: USGS Alberhill
Trail contacts: Cleveland National Forest, Trabuco Ranger District, 1147 East Sixth Street, Corona 92879; (951) 736-1811; www.fs.fed.us/r5/cleveland

Finding the trailhead: From Interstate 5 (Santa Ana Freeway) in San Juan Capistrano, drive approximately 23.1 miles east on the Ortega Highway (Highway 74). The El Cariso Ranger Station will be on the right (south). Parking is available directly in front of the visitor center. If this parking lot is full, park in the lot across the highway. The trail begins immediately to the right of the visitor center.

The Hike

This trail is a great way to familiarize yourself with some of the natural history of the Santa Ana Mountains. Stop at the small visitor center and, if available, pick up a trail pamphlet that is coordinated with numbered markers found along the trail. This pamphlet will help you identify some

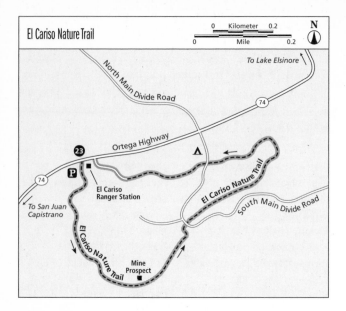

of the plants, animals, and geologic features of this coastal mountain range.

In spring a variety of wildflowers can be observed, along with a wide variety of coastal shrubs. The Coulter pines (called penny pines) have been planted over the years and are native to the area. Although there is some shade on the trail, most of the hike is exposed to the sun. Avoid this hike on hot summer days, or start early in the morning.

A small shaded area with tables is located at the trailhead, behind the visitor center; this is a perfect spot for a picnic.

The trail begins as a dirt path on the right (west) side of the visitor center. Head up stone steps, then proceed uphill under the oaks. Almost immediately you break out into scrub oak and coastal sage and head up a few short switchbacks.

Beyond a bench, the trail follows the contours of the western slope of the hill, offering expansive vistas. The trail climbs slightly and heads up a short section of stone steps. As the trail winds around to the southern side of the hillside, note the acorn-bearing scrub oak, which was a valuable food source for Native Americans.

At 0.4 mile (Signpost 10), an interesting old mine prospect (beginning of a mine shaft) and tunnel head into the hillside. To the south, you can gaze into the San Mateo Canyon Wilderness. The trail heads east, eventually reaching and crossing the paved South Main Divide Road. The trail continues east into scattered stands of Coulter pines and brings you to Signpost 12.

Intermittent shade and sun are encountered as the trail turns north and then west, reaching and crossing South Main Divide Road a second time at 1.2 miles. More open terrain behind picnic areas leads to a paved storage area. Continue across the storage area to your starting point.

Miles and Directions

0.0   Start on the dirt path to the right of the visitor center.

0.4   Pass the old mine prospect and tunnel.

1.2   Cross South Main Divide Road a second time.

1.4   Arrive back at the visitor center.

24 Morgan Trail

The Morgan Trail offers a great deal of variety for a short wilderness hike. The trail takes you from open chaparral to the shade of oaks, sycamores, and willows along Morrell Canyon Creek, then back up to views toward Sitton Peak in the west. Along the banks of Morrell Canyon Creek, large boulders and grassy areas shaded by ancient oak trees provide ideal spots for wildlife watching, sitting, daydreaming, or picnicking.

Distance: 4.5 miles out and back
Approximate hiking time: 2.25 hours
Difficulty: Moderate
Elevation gain: 500 feet
Trail surface: Smooth to rugged footpath
Best season: Fall through spring; early mornings in summer
Other trail users: None
Canine compatibility: Dogs not permitted

Fees and permits: Forest Adventure Pass required—$5 for day pass; $30 per year
Schedule: No set hours
Maps: USGS Alberhill, Sitton Peak
Trail contacts: Cleveland National Forest, Trabuco Ranger District, 1147 East Sixth Street, Corona 92879; (951) 736-1811; www.fs.fed.us/r5/cleveland

Finding the trailhead: From Interstate 5 (Santa Ana Freeway) in San Juan Capistrano, drive approximately 23.4 miles east on the Ortega Highway (Highway 74). Turn right (southeast) onto Killen Trail Road (South Main Divide Road) and drive 2.5 miles to the Morgan Trail parking area, which is on your right (south).

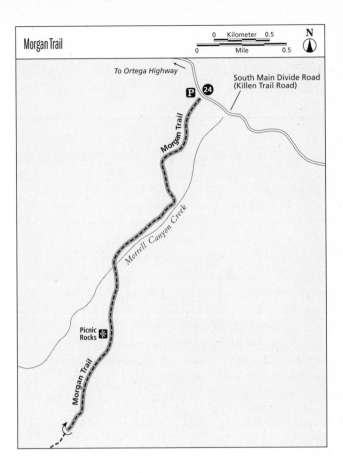

0   Kilometer   0.5

0   Mile   0.5

N

To Ortega Highway

South Main Divide Road
(Killen Trail Road)

P 24

Morgan Trail

Morrell Canyon Creek

Picnic
Rocks

Morgan Trail

The Hike

Like the Bear Canyon Trail (Hike 21), the Morgan Trail
takes you into the San Mateo Canyon Wilderness Area in
the southern part of the Santa Ana Mountains. In fact, with

a car shuttle between the Morgan and Bear Canyon trail-heads, you could make a point-to-point hike of 5.1 miles.

From the small parking area, head southwest as the trail gradually descends. After a short distance you will encounter a backcountry registration station. The trail continues a slight descent and at 0.2 mile reaches an oak woodland along Morrell Canyon Creek. Continue downstream on gentle rolling terrain along the right (northwest) side of Morrell Canyon under the shade of oaks that often arch across the trail. Note the many fire-scorched tree trunks.

As the canyon deepens, you will pass many granite rocks and boulders. The trail slowly enters more-open terrain and crosses Morrell Canyon Creek at 1.2 miles. Continue along the opposite side of the creek in open chaparral as the trail rolls slightly up and down. Some flat rocks on your right at 1.5 miles make a nice spot for a picnic, with open vistas to the west.

The trail heads down a moderate grade along a wide-open ridge toward the more level *poterra*, a Spanish word for a flat and open meadow. The trail levels and heads over some small ridges. At 2.2 miles you'll come to a fenceline and old fire road. Turn around at the fence, following the Morgan Trail back the way you came.

Miles and Directions

0.0   Start at the parking area on Killen Trail Road.

0.2   Reach Morrell Canyon Creek.

1.2   Cross Morrell Canyon Creek.

1.5   Arrive at a picnic area on flat rocks.

2.2   Reach the fence line and turnaround point.

4.4   Arrive back at the trailhead.

Language in the USA

Edited by CHARLES A. FERGUSON
Professor of Linguistics
Stanford University

SHIRLEY BRICE HEATH
Associate Professor of Anthropology and Education
Stanford University

with the assistance of DAVID HWANG

Foreword by DELL H. HYMES

CAMBRIDGE UNIVERSITY PRESS

CAMBRIDGE

LONDON   NEW YORK   NEW ROCHELLE

MELBOURNE   SYDNEY

Published by the Press Syndicate of the University of Cambridge
The Pitt Building, Trumpington Street, Cambridge CB2 1RP
32 East 57th Street, New York, NY 10022, USA
296 Beaconsfield Parade, Middle Park, Melbourne 3206, Australia

First published 1981

Printed in the United States of America

British Library Cataloguing in Publication Data
Language in the USA.
1. United States – Languages – History
I. Ferguson, Charles A II. Heath, Shirley
Brice III. Hwang, David
409'.73   P377   80-49985

ISBN 0 521 23140 X hard covers
ISBN 0 521 29834 2 paperback

Foreword

The United States is a more interesting country than it sometimes lets itself admit. One does not have to go to India or New Guinea for diversity of language. To be sure, it may sometimes seem that there are only two kinds of language in the United States, good English and bad. Only one kind, if some people are to be taken literally: English, surrounded by something else that cannot be called "English," or even perhaps "language." Yet within range of the broadcast in which such remarks are made may be households where there is knowledge of Spanish, Yiddish, Chinese, Korean, Vietnamese, Italian, German, Haitian, Ukrainian, Hebrew, and more. Driving through Arizona, the news on one wave length may be in Navajo. A church convention may be held partly in Finnish. Montana is the state of "big sky," and of fishing spots remote enough to find oneself alone, yet it is linguistically rich as well, as one chapter of this book reveals.

It is not that extermination of diversity has not had its advocates and successes. Many of the languages spoken in North America before Europeans came to its shores are dead. Many adults grew up in homes in which it would have been natural to become bilingual, but are monolingual today. Institutional policies and personal shame or fear of disadvantage have taken their toll. Whereas school children in Denmark and the Netherlands and elsewhere may grow up conversant with several languages, American school children usually pass through the stage of life in which it is easiest to learn languages without learning any beyond their first. Europeans see commercial, political, intellectual, and personal advantage in knowing the languages of other countries and cultures. Americans, somehow, seldom do.

Is it that we think the brain too small a place to hold more than one language at a time? That room for Spanish or Navajo will leave too little room for English? Is it that we fear that other ways of speaking will lead to an understanding of other ways of life, and so weaken commitment to our own? Is it perhaps that command of languages is assigned to a sphere of culture reserved for girls and women, something not suitable for boys and men?

Whatever the reasons, the United States is a country rich in many things, but poor in knowledge of itself with regard to language. That poverty has a cost. Laws and programs involving language are put into effect without much knowledge of the situations to be addressed. The civil rights movement stimulated

v

attention to the educational needs of Black children. Lack of adequate knowledge of the actual language situation led to mistaken efforts on the part of many, liberal and conservative alike. Much more is now generally known about features that may be characteristic of some Black speech, about styles of verbal interaction, and about attitudes toward such things on the part of Black people. Yet the initial stimulus to research has not been well sustained. The full scope of the language experience of Black Americans would richly repay further study; there is need for a greater number of Black scholars to contribute to such knowledge. Commitment to these goals has seemed to wax and wane with the national political climate. It has not been well established as a purpose in its own right, one that will prove invaluable when the concerns that led to the civil rights movement once again crest.

The bilingual education of Spanish-speaking Americans has followed a similar course. Political mobilization and regard for equity have led to programs which had little in the way of precedent and basic research on which to draw. Courts have mandated tests which no one had experience in devising. Again, the efforts of many Native Americans to preserve and revitalize their languages sometimes can draw on existing knowledge and skilled assistance, sometimes not. There have been universities in the United States for two hundred years, but there is still not a single chair devoted to such languages.

In general, one sees a recurrent pattern of a surge of attention to a language situation, because of social and political concerns, and then a lapse. Research follows, not the flag, but political forces, and then fades away.

I paint the picture too bleakly, perhaps; a number of contributors to this book work steadily to make the picture less true. Yet this book derives importance from the degree to which the picture is correct. It is the first book to address the situation of language in the United States as something to be known comprehensively and constantly to be better known. That fact is bittersweet. It makes one doubly glad for the work of editors and contributors, yet sad that until now a concerned citizen could not find such a book.

The book is first of all an account of the country's linguistic richness, in relation to issues that concern many citizens. Its existence, and the future to which it points, depend on constancy of scholarly effort to obtain, sift, and interpret such information. The editors and contributors are to be thanked especially for showing so abundantly that usable knowledge of the current language situation of the country is worthy of such effort. The greater part of the attention of linguists in recent years has gone to models of language in general, neglecting languages in particular. Where the particular forms of language in the United States have been studied, often enough the concern has been with what has been, not with what is or is coming to be. Dialects of English have been studied in terms of geographical isolation and Old World provenience; European languages spoken in the United States have been examined in terms of their relation to the language in Europe; Native American languages have been studied in terms of what was aboriginal and oldest. The current life of language in a community has been neglected. It is to be hoped that this book will herald increased attention to that life.